I0583663

TALES OF MUSIC AND MAGIC

ANTHEA SHARP

FIDDLEHEAD PRESS

CONTENTS

To all the Sharp musicians in my life.

INTRODUCTION

I grew up in a music-rich household, with a professional musician mother and a music aficionado father. My brother and I sang all the time to entertain ourselves, making up harmonies, changing the words to commercial jingles, and learning songs old and new. Since then, I've spent time as a professional fiddler and singer performing at Celtic music and folk festivals with my band Fiddlhead, and as a teacher, passing on the fiddle traditions to hundreds of students over the years.

I also grew up steeped in fantasy, devouring *Narnia* and *Lord of the Rings*, *The Dark is Rising* and *The Blue Sword*. When I started to write, I wrote the kind of stories I loved to read, full of fantastical worlds where magic is real and people struggle to master the powers given to them. So I suppose it's no surprise that music and magic are two threads that run strongly through many of my tales.

The idea that musicians can make magic has been around for centuries, if not longer. The tale spinners, minstrels, and bards have held respected places throughout history. Even now, our current musical stars create magic of a kind, speaking directly to the souls of their listeners, packing stadiums, making statements about life and what's important through their songs.

Recently, Celtic harps have dominated my stories. I didn't realize quite how *many* of my tales featured that particular instrument until I began putting together this collection. Perhaps it's because of the strong connection between bardic magic and the harp, or maybe it's the fault of the little lap harp currently residing in my music room, waiting for me to find time to play it. Whatever the case, brace yourself: harp tales are coming.

In addition to a plethora of Celtic harps, you'll find a cello, and an orchestra at the North Pole. Of course there's the music itself: pop songs, ballads, and symphonies, all with the power to make the world a better place. And what are we here for, if not to do that very thing? As artists, we strive to try and change things for the better, to bring solace and peace and hope. Especially in difficult times.

Music *is* magic. Listen, read, and believe.

～

INTO THE FAERIE HILL

I wrote this flash fiction piece for the NYC Midnight contest a few years ago. I made the semi-finals and had fun writing quickly to the prompts which, for this story, had to include the genre of historical fiction, an underground setting, and a bag of coins. Using that combo, I decided to explore a snippet of the legend surrounding the famous Irish harper Turlough O'Carolan (1670-1738), and how he came to be one of the most celebrated musicians of his time. Based on some historical evidence, whether or not the tale is true is for the reader to decide...

∾

Lough Scur, Ireland, 1690

CAROLAN STUMBLED over the knotted field, resenting the steadying arm of the servant, yet grateful to the man for keeping him from breaking his neck. The edge of autumn lay in the air, and the earthy smoke of peat. Every step released a dank whiff from the ground. Surely they must be near to the place.

"Is it dark yet?" he asked.

This was a thing best done under stars and moon, though he could not see them. Would never see anything again, since the fever had stolen his eyesight two years ago. He swallowed, glad of the flask in his pocket that helped keep the bitterness at bay.

"Sheebeg's just ahead," the servant said. "Watch yourself, lad—a gorse thicket here."

Picking through gorse was bad enough when one could see. Carolan bit his tongue on curses as the thorns scraped his skin and clawed at his coat.

They pressed through into a clear space, and the servant halted.

"The faerie hill," he whispered. "Are you certain—"

"Where's the entrance?" Carolan was not at all certain, but he'd given his word to spend the night.

In the morning he would wake raving with madness— or bearing the gifts of a bard.

Either one would be a welcome change.

The man led him forward a pace. "Best if you kneel."

Solid stone beneath his knees. Carolan reached, his fingers brushing slabs of lichen-knobbled rock shoring up the sides.

Directly before him lay emptiness, a passage into the hill. He could feel the exhalation of the earth against his face.

His salvation. Or his grave.

"Luck be with you," the servant said, unease tightening his voice.

Carolan nodded and the man retreated, the rustle of gorse marking his departure.

"Well, then," Carolan said to himself. He'd come too far to turn away now.

Ducking his head, he went into the ground.

The tunnel quickly narrowed until he was forced to go on his belly. Fear latched onto his spine. The flask in his pocket scraped against stone, and the bag of coins he'd brought clanked softly.

After what felt an eternity, but was only ten thundering beats of his heart, his head emerged into a larger space. He drew in a deep breath, his chest still constricted by the passage. Pray God he did not fall headlong into a cache of ancient swords or a battery of muskets. If he died here, he wished it would not be from clumsiness.

The floor proved to be less than a foot down. Carolan wriggled, sprawling ungracefully out of the passageway. One hand extended cautiously over his head, he sat up.

His fingers encountered a slab of stone, unbroken as far as he could reach.

"Ta!" he said sharply, listening for the space to throw the syllable back at him. No echoes came, confirming his sense he was in a small enclosure.

An enclosure he had no desire to explore further. Whether this was a military fortification or a barrow grave, he sensed danger.

Tis the provenance of the Fair Folk, his mind whispered. *You* should *be afraid.*

He fumbled the flask from his pocket and unstoppered it. Lifting it to his lips, he paused.

"To the spirits of this place," he said, "whatever you may be, I mean no harm. Accept this humble offering."

He reached into the blackness and poured out a libation. It splashed against stone, filling the chamber with sharp, sweet fumes.

The burn of the whiskey against his throat soothed him. Warmed him against the coming night.

"I've this, as well." He pulled out the sack of coins and placed it at the edge of the passageway. He prayed it might guard his sleep and appease the fey and fearful things that crept through the dark.

There was nothing else to do but finish the flask, then put the hard stone at his back and close his eyes.

The faerie folk chased through his dreams, wielding bright swords under the command of a giant chieftain and his warrior queen. Their armies danced together in starlight, the battle surging between two hills like the waves of the sea. A melody called to Carolan, full of sadness, full of joy. He followed it, his heart rising up like a white moth beneath the stars.

～

"TAKE CARE." The voice sounded into the darkness. "What if he's a madman?"

"Then you may club him. Carolan! Are you there, man?"

He woke, and nearly scrambled to his feet until he remembered he was in the depths of the hill.

"Hello?" he called, his throat fuzzy with sleep. "Squire Reynolds?"

The man who had challenged him to sleep beneath the faerie mound.

"A blind harper with little talent is a sorry thing, indeed," the squire had said. "Better to dare greatness and fail, than to continue on in mediocrity."

Carolan straightened from the rock, his mind awhirl with fey images, bound with melody. Was he mad?

"Go in," Squire Reynolds urged his servant. "See if he's alive."

"I'm here!" Carolan called.

He felt for the mouth of the passageway, and touched the bag of money. The hard, round coins were gone. Neck prickling, he stuck two fingers inside and touched something brittle and rustling. Faerie gold, changed into dry leaves by the light of day.

Carolan pocketed the bag and crawled through the passageway. Behind him came an ancient breath, carrying the whisper of a tune. Or madness.

The sharp scent of bruised gorse greeted him, and then Squire Taylor hauled him forth, exclaiming and brushing off his shoulders.

"Grave dust upon you, or worse," the squire said cheerfully. "So lad, which is it?"

The music brightened inside Carolan, like the sun burning through morning mist. A swirl of melody, where the faeries of the big hill and the faeries of the little hill strove together.

A tune that would carry him forward into the rest of his life.

"Bring me my harp," he said.

THE HARPER'S ESCAPE

Originally appearing in the Fiction River anthology Hidden in Crime, *this story is also based on the history of harpers in Ireland. It's a bit dark, perhaps, but then again, it deals with a grim time for the culture and people of Eire.*

BRONAGH O'RIADA DUG HER HEELS INTO HER MOUNT'S sides, then glanced over her shoulder. The road spooled out behind her, passing over green hills and through fields full of wild grasses. In the distance, a single standing stone poked up into a sky the color of pewter. The sun polished a bright spot in the west, but remained hidden behind the afternoon clouds.

No sign of the soldiers. Yet.

She pushed the hood of her cloak back, letting the wind pull at her silver-brown braid. Her harp, wrapped in its oilskin case, jolted uncomfortably against her back. Bron-agh's blessing—and her curse.

Until last year, the queen's edicts against harpers—though strongly worded—had been heeded by few. Bronagh had been left to go about her trade with little opposition. True, some of the lords had closed their doors in her face, but on the whole, she was still gladly received nearly everywhere she went.

And then Cromwell had invaded Ireland, with his soldiers and hatred, and fear rode over the countryside on dark hooves. A month ago, she'd fled the carnage at Drogheda, where she'd long found patronage with Lord and Lady Bray. But it was not safe, especially when word came that those who wished to curry Cromwell's favor were seeking her.

She'd turned north, toward the wilds of Ulster. Surely she'd be safe journeying past Lough Neagh and up into Antrim. But her music left a trail behind her like breadcrumbs.

Aye, and she should stop her playing, stop bringing light and tales and music to the hearths of noble parlors and common inns alike. But how could she, when she carried the unmistakable badge of her profession in the large, triangular case at her back? She had not trained in the bardic arts, nor accepted the mantle of a harpist, only to deny her tales and songs to the people who needed her most. And it was not in her nature to cower at the first hint of trouble.

Unfortunately, what pursued her was not the first hint of trouble, nor the second, nor even the third. This was death, breathing hard at her back, and Bronagh was afraid.

"Bide with us," Lady Bray had said, at their estate outside Drogheda. "We can keep you safe from Cromwell and his men."

"Thank you, my lady, but no." Bronagh had shaken her head. "Cromwell and his supporters are far too near—and my presence here cannot remain hidden. I'll not put you in danger by remaining here."

Already she had relied overlong on the Bray's hospitality.

"Where will you go?" Lady Bray had asked.

"I'll seek the road, and put half the length of Ireland between myself and the Pale."

She'd gratefully accepted the purse Lady Bray had bestowed upon her, and the gift of the swift-footed gelding, Dochas.

Even if she played and sang, she trusted she'd be able to stay ahead of any word sent back to the invaders. By the time Cromwell sent men to apprehend her, she would be gone.

But she had not expected the garrison of soldiers in Newry, or the man dining at the inn, who'd carried the tale of her presence to the garrison captain. Only the innkeeper's warning had enabled her to flee ahead of the approaching soldiers.

She leaned forward, patting her mount's lathered neck. They must find shelter soon.

Mouth twisting, Bronagh thought of the abandoned stone hut she'd spotted some miles back. Perhaps she ought to have tried to hide herself there. Or her harp, while she continued on.

But the idea of parting from her instrument was a knife driven deep into her heart. Without her harp, she was not a harper. Might as well cut off her two hands into the bargain.

Dochas stumbled, and Bronagh eased the reins, letting the horse slow. Overhead, the clouds thickened, the sunlight a pall over the land. Once more, she glanced back. A soft fog of dust rose over the green hillocks. She could not stop and rest—the soldiers were gaining on her.

The road rose, crossing a vein of granite, with boulders thrust up on either side. Dochas's hooves rang on the stone, and then the horse stumbled again, letting out a sharp whinny.

"What is it?" Bronagh asked, pulling him to a stop, but she feared she knew the answer.

She nimbly dismounted, then coaxed the horse to lift each foot in turn. As she'd guessed—his left hind foot was missing its shoe. She did not know where on the road he had lost it, and she could not turn about to search for it. Nor could she nail it back on, even if she found it.

With trembling hands, she set her mount's hoof back down, then patted his neck.

She was nearly out of time. How many more breaths remained to her before the noose tightened about her neck? The day suddenly seemed brighter, the soft air searing her lungs. All the memories of the people she had played for, all the notes spent from beneath her fingers, all the ballads and news she had carried, lodged in her throat until she could barely breathe.

But she would not give up. She would not halt in the middle of the dusty road and wait for her doom to catch up to her.

"Come along, then," she said, slipping the reins over Dochas's head and leading him past the rocky outcrop. Her heart sprang up in her chest when they rounded the far side and she spied a rough track leading away from the road.

"Just a bit farther," she murmured, turning onto the smaller road.

The peaceful track eased the scorch of fear in Bronagh's veins. Bees circled the wild red clover on the verge, and vetch tangled among the grasses. In another lifetime she would have paused for a while, unwrapped her harp, and played for the solace of wind and sky.

But fate chased hard at her heels, and she could not stop.

Bronagh smelled peat smoke, baking bread, and the musk of cattle, just as Dochas pricked up his ears. They crested a rise to see a humble farm spread out in the vale below. The farmhouse walls shone whitely, the thatched roof was bright with new straw. A barn, a storehouse, and pastures bounded by stone walls where cattle and sheep grazed completed the scene.

The sweetness of it brought tears to her eyes. She paused, took a deep breath, then turned to lead Dochas back toward the road. She could not bring Cromwell's soldiers to despoil this place.

"Hoy!"

A stout woman in homespun skirts and a red kerchief had emerged from the farmhouse and was waving vigorously.

"Do come down," she called. "We haven't had a harper in these parts for near on a year."

Once her profession was invoked, Bronagh could not turn away. At the least, she must explain her reasons before brusquely leaving.

Two children joined the woman, a boy and a girl, their voices high and excited. Bronagh led Dochas down into the farmyard.

"I cannot stay," she said. "Soldiers are searching for me even now."

The farmwife's eyes widened and she glanced at the track leading into the vale. Her gaze shifted to Bronagh.

"Then why are you not riding?" she asked.

"My horse threw a shoe."

And what wretched timing that had been. Not that Bronagh had imagined she could outride the soldiers. But still—she had hoped for another few hours of her life. Enough time to watch the long twilight fade into night before being taken.

"I fear there's no chance for me to bide." Bronagh scanned the rolling hills past the farm. "Is there anywhere beyond where I might shelter? A barrow, or hut?"

"No. We'll hide you here."

"Tis a crime to do so," Bronagh said.

The farmwife studied Dochas. "Then take your mount

into the barn. My husband will saddle one of our horses so that you might ride on."

"I can't steal one of your horses," Bronagh said.

The woman smiled at her. "Ah, 'tis but a loan. And besides, you'll be leaving your own horse here with us."

It was an unlooked for kindness. Bronagh swallowed past the catch in her throat.

"A blessing upon this house," she said.

The farmwife ruffled her son's brown hair. "Liam, run tell your father what's afoot."

He gave her a quick smile and sprinted to the outbuilding. His sister watched Bronagh with large, dark eyes.

"Aoife, take the harper to the barn," her mother said. "I'll fetch some bread and ale to travel on."

"My thanks," Bronagh said.

She forced herself not to scan the road. Every moment she remained at the farm put them all deeper in danger. But the farmwife was right—it was no use traveling with a lame horse.

"Is it hard?" the girl asked, nodding to the harp upon Bronagh's back.

"Yes, and no." Bronagh led Dochas to the barn, the girl beside her. "The harp has a pleasing tone of itself. Set it upon a stone, and the wind might coax a melody from the strings. Yet it takes years of practice to master the instrument, and to learn the ballads required of a bard."

The girl nodded. "Haven't seen a woman harper before."

Bronagh would wager the child hadn't seen many harpers at all, in the slim decade that surely comprised her life.

"Women can be bards, though it's not as common." Bronagh had chosen that path, and sometimes the ache of what might have been lay against her soul. Children of her own. A family. A man to hold her through the dark hours.

Although this way, she would leave no broken hearts behind when the soldiers took her.

The sweet smell of hay and animal sweat folded around Bronagh as she passed through the open doors into the shadowy cave of the barn. Two horses were housed in the nearby stalls. They pricked their ears, and one nickered softly as she led Dochas past.

"Da's back here," the girl said, skipping ahead.

A broad man rounded the horse he was saddling, and offered his calloused hand.

"I'm Aidan," he said, regarding her with the same solemn, dark eyes as his daughter. "We'll have Donn here ready for you in another moment. Liam, take her horse."

The boy sprang forward and Bronagh handed him the reins.

"Let me fetch my saddlebags," she said, as if she would have need of her possessions beyond that night.

She gently slid the straps of the harp case off her shoulders, so that she might move unburdened. Aoife watched, and Bronagh wished she had a little more time to unwrap the instrument and show the girl the beautifully carved knotwork soundbox, the wire strings that rang like bells when plucked with her sharpened nails.

"Hurry!" The farmwife hastened into the barn, a loaf in one hand and a flask of ale in the other. "Liam, go keep watch at the door."

Bronagh hefted her saddlebags over to her new mount and gave him a pat, then gratefully tucked away the provisions. She might have one last meal, and it would be the height of rudeness to refuse the farmwife's hospitality.

"Ma!" Liam sprinted back, his expression sharp with fear. "The soldiers have just come over the hill."

Bronagh's heart took up a heavy thumping, like a deep frame drum struck over and over with the beat of fear.

"Out the back?" she asked.

"No," the farmer said. "They'd see you and bring you down. Best if you hide in the straw."

"I'll go out and offer them some ale," his wife said. "Aoife, Liam, there never was a harper here, understand?"

"Aye," Liam said, and his sister nodded.

The farmwife shooed her children ahead of her, out into the pale afternoon light.

"They won't stop searching for me," Bronagh said to dark-eyed Aidan. "I'll not bring danger on your house."

"Let us at least try to turn them aside," he said, holding open a stall door for Dochas.

Bronagh led the horse inside, then gave the farmer a single nod. She would stay concealed in the barn. For now.

Aidan did not smile at her, but his eyes were warm with sympathy. Without another word, he strode out of the building. Bronagh took a deep breath. She rounded her mount, and laid her forehead against Dochas's, the rough hair tickling her skin.

"Thank you for bearing me so many miles," she whispered.

Then she went to her harp. Tucking it in the far corner,

she pulled a bag full of oats in front of the instrument. It was a rough concealment, but better than nothing. Her throat was too tight to bid her harp good bye. It was like saying farewell to her own heartbeat.

Quietly, she crept to the weathered barn doors and peered through a knothole in the wood.

The company of twelve soldiers clattered into the farmyard. Aidan and his wife met them, and the men eagerly accepted the jug of ale the farmwife offered. The captain questioned the farmer, who shook his head.

"No," Aiden said. "We've had no visitors. But come in and sit a while, if you'd like."

The captain narrowed his eyes and looked about the farmyard, and Bronagh shrank back into the shadows.

"Harper!" the man shouted. "If you are hiding here, no good will come of it."

She folded her hands, the tips of her nails biting sharply into her palms.

The captain gestured to one of his men. The soldier dug through his saddlebag and, to Bronagh's horror, produced three torches.

"I don't believe you," the captain said. He dismounted and took a torch in one gloved hand. "Set fire to the barn, men. If the vermin is hiding there, we'll smoke her out. And if not, let the building burn as the penalty for lying to soldiers. There's no place else she could have gone. Unless you've something to confess?" The captain turned to Aidan.

"No." The farmer folded his arms.

His wife gave him an anxious look, but said nothing.

Bronagh quieted the protests filling her mouth, and waited. Perhaps the soldiers were only bluffing.

One of the junior officers produced flint and tinder, and soon all three torches were smoking. As soon as the bright bloom of flame appeared, the captain strode toward the barn and bent, letting the fire lick at the corner of the door.

He was so near, Bronagh could see the sweat upon the side of his neck.

"Wait," she said, moving from her concealment. The stench of burning tar made her eyes burn. "I am the harper you seek."

"No!" the girl, Aoife, cried, but her mother caught her arm and pulled her close.

"I thought as much." The captain took her wrist in his hard grasp, and held her hand up for inspection.

The pointed tips of her fingernails were damning evidence that she was a harper, and the man made a grunt of satisfaction. Half of his company surrounded Bronagh, while the others kept watch on Aidan and his family.

She felt a morbid smile stretch her lips. A dozen soldiers, to capture one harper? What a dangerous creature she was. The men watched her, their eyes as hard as stones.

"Where is your harp?" the captain demanded.

She stared into his eyes, and summoned every ounce of her bardic arts.

"I left it at the inn in Newry," she said. "I knew it would be safe there, with you so hot to follow my trail."

His lips turned down, and she knew she'd found her mark. They hadn't bothered to search the inn, once word of her flight reached them. And they could hardly return now to verify her story.

"Search the farmhouse, and the barn," he called to his men.

Bronagh smiled. "By all means, please do. I am not so eager to meet the noose, after all. And 'tis a pleasant afternoon. I'll gladly bide here a while."

"Wait!" the captain barked, and the men at the door of the farmhouse hesitated.

"Don't let me stop you," Bronagh said, her voice all pleasantness.

He scowled at her, and beckoned to his closest soldier.

"Bind her," he said. "It's growing late, and we should return to Newry."

"But, sir," one of his men said. "What about the family?"

"Leave them," the captain said. The burning torch he still held smudged the air with soot.

He watched, face set, as his men bound Bronagh's wrists, then pushed her up onto a horse before of one of the soldiers. The man clasped her against him, his arm like steel.

She did not protest or struggle—there was no use for it. The shadowy form of death grew ever closer, but she was determined to meet it with dignity.

"Mount up," the captain commanded.

As soon as his men were ready, he strode to the barn door and tossed the flaming torch inside. The dry straw caught fire instantly, and smoke billowed from the door. The horses began to whinny in their stalls, and Bronagh prayed the flames would not consume the building before Aidan could save his horses. And Dochas.

As for her harp, it would burn, or not, but she would never again hold it against her shoulder and let the music ring forth. Still, she could not bear the thought of it burning; the wood blackening, the strings snapping and curling in the fire.

"Your punishment, for aiding the harper," the captain said to Aidan as he swung up into the saddle. "Be grateful it is so light."

Bronagh shot a glance at the farmer and his family. They stood in a huddle beside the farmhouse, and were wise enough to say nothing. Flames crackled inside the barn, the horses whinnied desperately, but Aidan kept his gaze fixed on the soldiers.

Young Aoife's eyes met hers, and Bronagh sent a silent wish that the girl recover the harp from the burning barn, and tend it well. If only the soldiers would *go*.

"Away!" the captain cried.

The thud of hooves up the road masked the roar of flames. At the crest of the hill, Brea glanced over her shoulder. Aidan and his family had sprung into action, and she saw Aoife's small shape dart into the barn, despite her father's cry of protest.

The soldier she was riding with cuffed her head.

"Eyes forward," he said.

Temple aching from the blow, she turned her face to the road. Behind them, a black plume of smoke rose on the wind. Ahead, the sun hurried toward the west, the clouds shredding away to at last to reveal a blazing sky. Between the two, the harper rode to meet her end. It was nearly enough for the makings of an epic song.

But there would be no one to sing it.

Bronagh forced her heart to silence as they traveled, the long miles stretching into twilight. Her shoulders ached, and her neck was cold, the shadow of the noose upon it.

At the smudged edges of the horizon, the first stars began to shine. The last stars she would ever see.

Closing her eyes, Bronagh let the darkness take her.

Her soul grew still, the songs fled from her lips, and her heartbeat faded. Dimly, she heard the captain call a panicked halt, but she was already gone, stepping over the threshold between one existence and the next.

The last thing she heard was the chiming of a harp—the notes borne on a wind from beyond the mortal world. A wild melody, full of grief, full of joy.

She followed the music home.

THE QUIET GIFT

This tale was first published in Crucible: All-new Tales of Valdemar, *and is reprinted here with the kind permission of Mercedes Lackey. Set in her world of Velgarth, at the Collegium where Gifted students go to study, this story examines the problem of ambition and talent getting in the way of actual musicality.*

SHANDARA TEM LET THE LAST CHORD RING FROM HER HARP, the notes filling Master Bard Tangeli's office with triumphant sound.

The crackling fire on the hearth was the only sound in the room besides the final notes. Master Tangeli sat in his armchair, fingers steepled beneath his neatly trimmed gray beard. He did not smile, did not move from his pensive pose.

As the last vibrations faded from the harp, Shandara's

smile faded from her face, too. "Did you...like my new composition?"

She had hoped for more. A nod of approval from her instructor at least, if not warm applause. Anything but this studied silence.

"Valor" was one of her best compositions. She knew it was—an homage to the bards of yore and their service to Valdemar. Surely it was good enough to convince the Bardic Council to elevate her from Trainee to full Bard. Already several of her friends had donned their Scarlets and left Haven, leaving her increasingly impatient to do the same.

A flurry of snowflakes danced past the windows, and the golden glow of the lamps warmed the intricately patterned carpet beneath Shandara's feet. The weight of the harp was comforting against her right shoulder as she waited. And waited.

At last, Master Tangeli spoke. "The melodic line is lovely. Very well suited to your soprano voice—and the interweaving chords lend a strong backdrop to your lyrics. Especially the minor to major substitutions. But... something is missing. As I'm sure you are aware."

Failure settled coldly in the pit of her stomach, as though she'd swallowed a lump of ice.

"I'm trying, Master," she said. "Surely you felt some excitement as you listened?"

"I felt moved by your talent, certainly." He shook his head. "But not by your Gift."

Shandara took a deep breath, swallowing the discouraged lump in her throat. It wasn't professional to cry in front of one's instructor, and she refused to do so.

But it also wasn't fair. She had done *everything* in her power to evoke the emotions of her song; tried her utmost to activate her Bardic Gift and let it carry that sense of honor and triumph to her audience.

"I'd hoped this would be the piece," she said softly, running her right hand up and down the smooth pine of her harp's soundbox.

"It is a strong composition," Master Tangeli said. "Very complex. And though I know you are disappointed, promise me you'll perform at the Midwinter Recital next week."

She dropped her gaze to the carpet. Could she bear to debut her new song before the Collegium, and have it meet with failure?

"Perhaps the energy of playing before a large audience will unlock your sporadic Gift more fully," her instructor added.

That was the maddening part. Shandara *had* the Bardic Gift, but it was so elusive! Before she'd come to the Collegium, she had made her younger siblings dance and laugh or weep bitterly, depending on the song she played. She'd been so certain that her prodigious talents would earn her full Bard status and her Scarlets at a remarkably early age.

Instead, she'd seen most of her yearmates depart for positions in noble houses, while she remained behind. Still a Trainee.

She'd always been a talented musician—one of the best

harpers he'd ever seen, Master Tangeli had told her. But the harder she worked, the less reliable her Gift became.

"Very well," she said. "I'll perform at the recital." It was not as though she could refuse her instructor's request.

"Good." He nodded. "Tomorrow, we'll go over the transition into the chorus. It is the only thing I heard that needs work—the rest of your piece is excellent. Well done, Shandara."

"Thank you," she said, hearing his unspoken words.

Well done... but not quite well enough.

Glumly, she wrapped her harp back in its thick cloth case and bid Master Tangeli good evening. She would go back to her room and work on the music until her fingers bled, if that was what it took to reach her Bardic potential.

Someone in a nearby practice room was playing a difficult run of notes on the gittern, over and over. To Shandara's ear, there was no improvement from one try to the next. Much like her attempts to master her Gift.

As she trudged up the stairs to the third floor dormitory, the dinner bell rang. Not that she was hungry—but if she didn't make at least a token appearance, her friend Ryk would worry. He fretted entirely too much about her, and now that most of their yearmates were gone, he fussed at her even more.

Her chest tightened with the knowledge that he would likely receive his Scarlets soon. Maybe even after the Midwinter Recital. And then she would be completely alone.

Oh, stop it, she told herself. Self-pity was no use to

anyone, and she didn't begrudge Ryk his inevitable success. It was just that she was going to miss him when he went.

Her room smelled of beeswax candles and the dried herbs strewn inside her mattress. The familiar scent soothed her, taking the edge off her unhappiness.

Dinner would help, too—and perhaps there would be pocket pies. She could do with a little sweetness in her day. Shandara tucked her harp into its corner beside her bed, then turned and went back down to brave the cold courtyard.

She waited inside the Bardic College's entryway for a moment or two, to see if Ryk would come, but there was no sign of him. Likely he'd already headed over to the dining hall. Their schedules did not often mesh, but she knew he would save a seat for her.

The cold air stung her face and stole her breath the moment she stepped out into the deepening twilight. A few snowflakes drifted past her, but the afternoon flurries seemed to have passed.

Across the stone-paved yard, the larger Herald's College was a comforting bulk, its many windows glowing golden. Shandara hunched her shoulders against the bitter wind and increased her pace, her fingers already chilled.

...Shandara...

It was a whisper on the wind, accompanied by a sleet-filled gust. Shandara whirled, then lost her footing on a treacherous patch of ice. Snow blinded her, and she cried out, arms windmilling in a vain attempt to regain her balance.

"No!"

She pulled in a panicked breath, the cold air invading her lungs. Her feet slid out from under her, and down she went on the unyielding paving stones.

She landed hard on her right side. Bright pain blossomed through her arm and shoulder and she lay there a moment, stunned. Snowflakes gathered on her lashes, pricked her cheeks.

"Shandara!" One of the third-year trainees rushed over. "Are you all right?"

"I think...I need a Healer," Shandara blinked back the tears of pain blurring her vision.

In what seemed like moments, she was surrounded by a circle of concerned faces. Some were lit by the glow of the Collegiums' windows, others were shadowed. The chill of the paving stones seeped into her body, but her shoulder hurt so badly she was not certain she could sit up.

"Should we move her?"

"Wait for Healer Adrun."

"Let me through!" That was Ryk. He knelt beside her, his brown eyes wide. "Shan, what happened? Where did you land? Did you break anything?"

His breath sent a frosty plume into the darkening air. Shandara managed a weak smile, then regretted it as her arm pulsed with pain.

"I tripped," she said. "Fell on my right side. Maybe broken." Her voice cracked on the last word.

It was a musician's worst fear; the thought of injuring a hand or arm, and being unable to play. While it was true the Healers at the Collegium were some of the best in the land, they could not mend every injury. At least, not instantly.

"Here." Ryk pulled off his cloak and folded it into quarters. "Can you lift your head?"

"You'll be cold," she said.

"You're the one lying on the stones. Hush now." He slipped the makeshift pillow under her cheek. The wool was rough against her skin, and smelled faintly of wood smoke.

"Make way." Master Tangeli pushed through the crowd, his lips pressed together with concern. "Give her some space."

"Indeed," a deep voice said. "Everyone, move over."

The crowd surrounding Shandara shifted as Master Healer Adrun strode to her. His emerald green clothing was a bright contrast to the rust and scarlet hues of the bards. He knelt on the icy stones, then held his hand over her body and closed his eyes in concentration.

"Well, young lady," he said after a moment, opening his eyes. "You've torn your shoulder and fractured your forearm. That was quite a fall. Glad you didn't hit your head—those are always difficult injuries to heal. Let's get you inside where it's warm. Then a round of Healing. Sit up—carefully. There you go."

Ryk moved to her left side and supported her as she unsteadily rose to her feet. At least the snow had lessened somewhat, the flakes now swirling gently around her, as if in apology.

Master Tangeli nodded at her. "I'll be in to check on you soon, Shandara. I hope your injury is not too grievous."

He raised his voice. "Everyone, thank you for stopping—but the cooks won't be happy if we are all late to dinner."

The crowd dissipated, leaving Shandara, Ryk, and Master Adrun to head back to the bard's dormitory. Slowly, with much wincing on her part, they managed the journey up to the third floor.

"Sit on the edge of the bed," Master Adrun said. "Easy, now. That's it."

Shandara breathed shallowly and stared at her colorful quilt, trying to calm herself so that Master Adrun could work with her body's natural energy flow. Still, her mind would not stop leaping from pain to fear to worry, then circling back again.

"Will I be well enough to perform at the Midwinter Recital?" she asked as the Healer held his hands above her shoulder. "I play the harp," she added, in case he did not know.

Master Adrun shot a glance at the instrument in the corner. "Harp? That takes a much larger range of motion than, say, a flute." He frowned. "You've torn a tendon, I'm afraid. Even with Healing, I have to advise two weeks of rehabilitation. It's unlikely you'll be able to play much of anything before then."

"But, I have to—"

"If you attempt to use your shoulder too soon, you could permanently weaken the joint, making you vulnerable to future injuries." He shook his head. "Not a risk a Bard should take."

He was right, though she hated to admit it.

"But you can still sing," Ryk said with an encouraging

smile. "You can accompany yourself with your left hand, and just let your right arm rest in your lap. Think of it as a challenge. You can show the Bardic Council that you can overcome obstacles and still perform."

"I suppose. But my composition depends on the interplay of left and right hand, as well as my voice. There's no way I can perform 'Valor.'"

"It's your piece," Ryk said. "I'm certain you can come up with a new arrangement."

His faith warmed her, and steadied her conviction. She could do it, re-work the song. The vocal part would have to carry the piece, but she had an excellent voice. And it would prove to the Council that she was a flexible musician, able to adapt to the unexpected; surely a most desirable quality in a Bard.

"Take a deep breath and hold it," Master Adrun said.

Shandara bit her lip at the flash of pain in her right shoulder.

"I've done what I can for now," the Healer continued. "For the next two days, keep your shoulder as immobilized as possible. I'll send a sling over, and will be back to check your progress tomorrow. For now, rest. And don't forget to eat. You'll find yourself quite tired from the Healing."

"I'll bring you a tray," Ryk said.

"Thank you." She gave her friend a grateful smile. Already, as Master Adrun had predicted, weariness washed over her.

As soon as they left, Shandara lay back on her bed. Her shoulder throbbed, but it was not the same searing pain as when she'd fallen on the courtyard stones. She closed her eyes for a moment, and it seemed that between one breath and the next, Ryk was there.

He helped her sit, and held the tray for her while she awkwardly spooned up her stew with her left hand. As soon as she finished, she yawned, her eyes lidded with lead.

"Good night," Ryk said with a smile, standing and taking up the tray. "I'll see you tomorrow."

"Night."

His sympathetic smile never leaving his face, he closed the door quietly behind him. Stifling another yawn, Shandara pulled the quilt over herself with her left hand. Undressing just then would be too difficult. Tomorrow, Genna could help her. But now sleep sang its sweet, compelling song to her. She followed that melody down into the warm dark.

"I can't believe it." The words came out in a croak. Shandara blew her nose for the hundredth time, and regarded Ryk glumly over the curve of her harp.

The candles on her dresser flickered gaily, in sharp contrast to her mood, and already she wished she could crawl under the covers and stay there until morning. She did not know how she could possibly get through the Midwinter Recital.

"Don't even try to speak," Ryk said. "You sound dreadful, like a swamp frog. I'll go tell Master Tangeli you won't be performing tonight."

"I have to," she whispered. "A Bard doesn't go back on her promises."

She'd given her instructor her word. Not once, but twice, reassuring him after her injury that she was still going to play at the recital.

Ryk shook his head, his shaggy brown hair falling into his eyes. "Everyone will understand. Not only are you playing one-handed, but now you've lost your voice!"

"It's my last chance."

She couldn't bear to watch Ryk don his Scarlets and leave. It wasn't absolutely certain that he would, of course. But Master Tangeli had strongly hinted that all the senior Trainees who performed at the Midwinter Recital had an excellent chance of earning their Full Bard status. Shandara suspected it was why he'd extracted her promise to perform.

And perform she would. If she could not dazzle the council with her musical ability, she would impress them with her sheer determination.

Despite her bravado, her stomach knotted at the thought. Her best chance had always been to amaze the Master Bards with her skillful harp playing and talented singing. Now, with her injured shoulder and croaking voice, she had neither.

She was reduced to plucking chords and humming. It was humiliating—but she would bear it. Better five minutes of wretchedness on stage than to be the last of her yearmates still at the Collegium.

"But what will you play?" Ryk frowned. "You could accompany me, if you'd like."

She shook her head. It was kind of him to offer, and she was certain she could fit in a bass line to his gittern playing, but in her heart, she knew that would be cheating. Besides, she didn't want to hurt Ryk's chances of advancement to full Bard status.

Whatever she played tonight, she'd have to take the stage alone.

"I'll manage," she whispered.

"I need to get ready," Ryk said. "Should I ask Genna to come help you dress?"

Shandara nodded. She had a russet gown with bright embroidery at the hem and sleeves that she would not be able to don one-handed.

"All right." Ryk gave her a careful hug. "And if you change your mind, let me know."

She smiled at him. "See you in the hall," she whispered.

As soon as he left, she turned her attention back to her harp. Worry scrabbled at her mind with sharp claws, but she pushed it away. She must think of *something* to perform.

She began plucking chords—a simple line that reminded her of a lullaby her mother used to sing. Experimentally, Shandara hummed the melody. What emerged from her throat was an odd, nasal sound, but for some reason she could make more sound with her mouth closed than when she tried to sing.

It was closer to the noise a bee would make than an actual singing voice, and she winced at it. But she must play. Even though this rough, half-accompanied lullaby would win her no prizes. And no Scarlets, either.

But she had promised Master Tangeli.

So, then. Grimly, she bent her head and began to hum. At least her left hand played true, moving smoothly through the chord changes. She even managed a little echo of the melodic line at one point. It would have to do, though her performance would be as raw and basic as any first-year Trainee's attempt.

FROM HER PLACE at the side of the stage, Shandara looked out over the assembled listeners. The hall was decked with greenery and candles, the audience a kaleidoscope of gray and rust, moss green and blue. Where the Master Bards sat, bright Scarlet grouped in clusters like holly berries, and a dazzling white splash in the middle of the throng denoted the Heralds. Here and there, the emerald of the Healers dotted the crowd. Shandara saw Master Adrun sitting with his peers.

He had visited earlier that day, repossessed his sling, and cautioned her to spend at least two more weeks doing the gentle exercises he had given her before trying anything more strenuous. She sighed and lifted her right arm two inches, stopping when she felt a twinge. If only her injury had been simpler to Heal.

Onstage, a fourth-year Trainee was just finishing her piece, a flute arrangement of one of the Vanyel Song Cycle ballads. The audience applauded, and Bard Vivaca, the master of ceremonies for the evening, announced the next performer.

"Ryk Tayard," she said. "Playing his own composition, 'Bright Dancer.'"

Holding his gittern by the neck, Ryk strode on stage, bowed, then sat on the stool set out for the performers. He gave his strings a quiet strum to check their tuning, tweaked one of the pegs, then lifted his head and began.

A flourish of notes leaped from beneath his fingers, and Shandara nodded, her foot tapping in time to the sprightly rhythm. Ryk had composed the piece after watching the Companions in their field one summer afternoon. They had known he was there, and had shown off, tossing their silvery manes and racing like streaks of light back and forth over the green summer grasses.

She could see them in her mind, evoked by Ryk's Gift. A flash of blue eyes, the high whinny that almost sounded like laughter, the warm confidence that, as long as the Companions and their Heralds rode the land, all would be well.

When Ryk finished, the applause was loud and long. To no one's surprise, the Heralds were most enthusiastic, calling out their approval. Ryk bowed, and Shandara's stomach tightened.

Her turn.

The concert was supposed to build to the most advanced student, and she wished that they had put her much earlier, with the first or second-year students. But no —she was last. And what an anticlimactic ending it would be.

"Shandara Tem, playing 'Evening Lullaby,'" Bard Vivaca said.

Forcing a smile onto her face, Shandara stepped onto the stage. At least she was able to carry her harp by herself, although a bit awkwardly. She set the instrument down before the stool and then took a seat.

A few of the students leaned over, whispering to their friends. She could imagine what they were saying—what a pity that Shandara was reduced to performing a basic lullaby, how embarrassing it must be for her...

Her cheeks flamed, and she squeezed her eyes closed for a moment, trying to focus. She was not sitting in the center of a stage, in the palace, in Haven. Instead, she imagined she was home: the bright braided rug in the center of the living room, the smell of smoke curling up from the hearth, her mother stroking her hair back from her forehead.

Shandara opened her eyes, set her left hand to her harp, and played the introductory line. Just a simple pattern of five notes. Nothing flashy, nothing even close to demonstrating her talent. At the end of the introduction, she began to hum. The harp sang under her hand, the chords ringing out and supporting the raspy tone swelling from her throat.

The wood vibrated against her shoulder, and she breathed, letting that feeling settle all through her until her entire body was an instrument, a vessel for the song. There was nothing else she could do—she was not concentrating on difficult fingering, or infusing words with emotion. There was only the simple pentatonic melody. So unimpressive she nearly wanted to weep.

She did not dare to look at the audience and see their

pitying looks. Instead, she thought of the twilight sky, orange and russet at the western horizon. The first, diamond-bright stars winking in the deeper velvet over-head. The soft brush of sleep at the end of a long and satis-fying day.

The audience was quiet. Too quiet.

Shandara risked a glance up, and her hand faltered over the strings. The entire front row, and the second, and the third, had their eyes closed and seemed to be asleep. Farther back in the audience, people were yawning and resting their heads on their friends' shoulders.

She was putting the entire Collegium to sleep. Was this buzzing resonance she felt inside of her the full manifesta-tion of her Bardic Gift?

She could not believe it. It was too simple. Yet the proof lay before her, slipping into slumber even as she watched.

At the end of the last phrase, Shandara let the harp strings ring instead of damping them with her hand. Slowly, the last thread of sound faded into the quiet hall. Only a few people remained awake—most of the Heralds, Healer Adrun, and the Master Bards. They watched her, varying expression of surprise or satisfaction on their faces. The rest of the audience snored on, showing no signs of waking.

Oh no! She had never made a single person fall asleep, let alone a hall full of listeners. What now?

She sent a panicked glance to Master Tangeli, and he waved his hand in a circle, motioning her to play more. Shandara drew in a deep breath of understanding. Much as she wanted to creep off the stage and leave everyone slumbering through the night, it was not an option. Her music had made them sleep, and so her music must rouse them.

No matter how embarrassed she would be when they awoke. Imagine—putting the entire Collegium and court to sleep. She would never live it down.

So then, she would play something lively. A jig. Cautiously, she raised her right hand, just high enough to reach the strings. Her shoulder did not complain as she plucked out the melody. As long as she confined her motion to one small area, she could manage.

The lilting tune floated over the audience, and Shandara added her left hand in a percussive bass line. The candle flames danced, and the crowd began to stir. Feet thumped in rhythm, and then a few people started to clap. Soon, the room was awake again, nearly everyone clapping along. Luckily, the Bards had good rhythm, and were able to keep even the most random members of the audience in time.

Shandara brought the tune to a close, and the rhythmic clapping diffused into true applause. From his seat among the Master Bards, Master Tangeli nodded at her. She could not meet his gaze.

"Thank you all for attending the Midwinter Recital," Master Vivaca called, striding onto the stage. "What a night of entertainment! Please join the Bards for refreshment in the Common Room."

Shandara clumsily picked up her harp and hurried offstage. Her shoulder ached, her temples throbbed, and her throat felt rough and scratchy. Above the heads of the milling audience, she saw Ryk searching for her. She could not stand his sympathy—not now, when he'd ended the evening in triumph, and she'd fumbled so badly.

Head down, she wrapped up her harp and hurried into the quiet halls. No one stopped her as she left the palace. The cold night air grabbed her breath, and she slowed down as she traversed the icy stones of the courtyard. Overhead, the stars were hard and brilliant, a scornful light that cared not for human fears and foibles.

The lamps flickered as she stepped inside the Bardic College, and the air was hushed. Letting the solitude wrap around her like a blanket, she slowly went up the stairs to the shelter of her room. Exhaustion crashed over her like a wave. She lay down and a moment later was asleep.

Through her dreaming, she was dimly aware of Ryk cracking her door open and holding up a light.

"Yes, she's here," he said to someone behind him in the hall.

The door closed again, leaving her in the solace of the dark once more.

WHEN SHANDARA FINALLY WOKE, sunlight filtered through the homespun curtains to form a wide band of bright light across the wooden floor. She took a deep breath and sat up, relieved to find her aches much abated. She swallowed, and realized she was parched.

And ravenous.

"Shandara?" Ryk tapped softly on her door. "Are you up?"

There was a happy note in his voice that told her he had cause to rejoice, and for a cowardly moment she almost didn't answer. But that was selfish—of course she would help him celebrate the fact that he'd gained his Scarlets.

"One moment," she called, her voice still raspy but not the croak of the day before. Hastily, she pulled on her clothing, then ran a brush through her hair. Feeling marginally presentable, she called for Ryk to enter.

He burst in, a wide grin on his face. As she had suspected, he was wearing bright red—his customary leather vest now worked in scarlet, his breeches colorful and bright.

"Look at you!" Careful of her still-mending shoulder, Shandara hugged him, then stepped back. She smiled, rejoicing in her friend's promotion, and pushed down the prick of envy in her heart. "Congratulations—I knew you could do it."

"I still don't quite believe it," he said, grinning bright enough to rival the sunlight. "Oh, I brought you some breakfast."

"You did?" The pang in her heart returned. Havens, she would miss him when he left.

Nodding, he stepped into the hall, and returned with a tray holding oatmeal, tea, and a fresh-baked scone. Her stomach rumbled in anticipation.

"Tell me," she said, accepting the tray and sitting on the bed, "when did you get your Scarlets? After the concert?" She took a bite of scone, the pastry still warm in the middle, despite being carried across the courtyard.

"Yes," Ryk said. "Master Tangeli presented them to me. He was looking for you, too, but you'd disappeared."

"I wasn't feeling well." No doubt he had something to say to her about how poorly she'd controlled her gift.

"You're better now, though?" Ryk still looked concerned. "Make sure to finish your oatmeal. Using the Gift takes a lot of energy, you know."

"Using it as awkwardly as a raw beginner, you mean." Shandara sighed. "I put the entire Collegium to sleep."

"Indeed." Master Tangeli spoke from the open doorway, a bundle tucked beneath his arm. "May I come in?"

"Please do." Inwardly, she cringed.

She'd avoided her scolding last night, but it was time for the reckoning. And why Ryk sat there with his smile broadening, she could not imagine.

"As you might expect," her instructor said, "I am here to deliver a lecture—and some words of advice. But before I do, I have something else to give you."

"Stand up, Shan," Ryk said, grabbing her tray and setting it aside.

A thin flicker of hope started up in Shandara's chest. *Oh, but surely not...*

"Shandara Tem," Master Tangeli said, his tone official, "it gives me great pleasure to present you with these."

He held out the bundle he'd been carrying. She took it, with effort keeping her hands steady, and slowly unwrapped the brown cloth covering. At the first glimpse of bright red silk, tears sprang to her eyes.

"Truly?" she whispered, pulling out the colorful shirt. It seemed she had earned her Scarlets after all.

"Welcome to the ranks of the full Bards, Shandara," her instructor said.

"Despite everything," she said, her voice catching on the words.

Master Tangeli's gray brows rose. "Despite? Or perhaps because of it. Having your immense musical skill dampened was quite likely the best thing that could have happened. It forced you to stop relying solely on your ability, and play from the heart."

"It seems so…contrary," she whispered.

"The Gift has its own rules," her instructor said. "Now, you must learn to play by them."

TWO DAYS LATER, Shandara was almost too nervous to eat a bite at breakfast—which was ridiculous. She was not the one leaving the Collegium. She took a sip of tea, and glanced across the table at Ryk.

"Do you have everything?" she asked. "Did the kitchens pack you some food? What about extra strings?"

He laughed at her, his brown eyes bright. The new scarlet shirt he wore complimented his coloring, although it was not silk like her own, but the rougher, homespun fabric he preferred.

"Shan, Lord Wendin's house is only across the city. It's not like I'm going far away. For once, you sound like me. Stop worrying."

She made a face at him, suddenly shy. "I know. It's just —I'll miss you."

"I'll come visit every week. But are you certain you'll be happy here?" He gestured to the Common Room full of trainees and Bards.

Shandara turned her head, looking at the tables filled with students, hearing the laughter and discontent, the rustling murmurs of the melodies of each life.

"Yes. I'm glad to be staying." She smiled.

She had thought her dream was to earn her Scarlets, then leave Haven, or at least the Collegium. She had thought her future was playing for some Lord's household while she composed, or perhaps traveling for a time, chronicling the adventures of the Heralds and their Companions.

But Master Tangeli had offered her a place as his assistant teacher. To everyone's surprise—including her own—she had accepted.

"It just feels right," she said. "I need the time and quiet to work on refining my Gift. And I think I can help other students find their own."

Ryk smiled at her, the corners of his eyes crinkling. "I have no doubt of it, Bard Shandara. No doubt at all."

~

THE CLOCKWORK HARP

Another story first appearing in a Fiction River collection,
Haunted, *this tale is a spooky retelling of the old ballad of the*
Cruel Sister. To twist things up even more, I've set it in my
Victoria Eternal universe, a world where technology and
Victorian sensibilities combine in a steampunk-like Space Opera
setting. You can find similar adventure in my new novel, Star
Compass.

MISS ELEANORA THOMAS WAS NOT FOND OF THE NEW
instrument her mother had proudly installed in the
drawing room three days earlier. It stood, a strange
marriage of wood and metal, in the center of the plush
Turkish carpet, directly in front of the bow window, where
the harpsichord had used to reside.

Eleanora sat with her mother, Lady Thomas, on the
plushly upholstered davenport, going over the day's corre-

spondence. There were the usual invitations to parties and balls, all of which Eleanora was expected to attend. She would rather continue working on the new clockwork butterfly she was constructing than be paraded about on the Spring Season marriage mart, but as the eligible daughter of a viscount, she had little choice in the matter.

"Well!" Her mother held up a note decorated with scrollwork. "The Eldwins are holding a ball to celebrate their daughter Anne's engagement next week. We shall attend, of course."

An odd, barely audible hum emanated from the soundbox of the harp. Eleanora glanced at her mother, but Lady Thomas seemed too engrossed in perusing her letters to notice the faint shimmer of sound.

Still, Eleanora slid a trifle closer to her mother and gave the instrument a sidelong look. The harp itself was unobjectionable. It was made of wood with gilt embellishments, strung with gut, and had a very pretty curve at the top. The ornately carved pillar was nearly as tall as Eleanora, who was admittedly on the petite side.

"So sad, about the younger sister," Lady Thomas continued. "But it's good to see families moving on. After an appropriate mourning period, of course."

The harp emitted another low sigh.

"Did you hear that?" Eleanora asked.

"I think you ought to wear your new gown," her mother said. "The one with the lifters. The style is all the rage, ever since the queen debuted it. Perhaps it will help you catch the eye of a worthy gentleman."

Eleanora was not particularly interested in catching the

eye of a worthy gentleman. She suspected the unworthy ones were far more interesting. Sadly, at the advanced age of eighteen, she had little experience with members of the opposite sex, besides dancing and making desultory conversation with them. The things that truly interested her were not suitable topics for a young lady of good breeding.

Her parents, of course, did not know of her work. They thought the hours she spent in her room were passed in reading and painting watercolors of flowers, when in fact the watercolors were dashed out as quickly as possible so that she might fashion miniature clockwork creatures. Some day, perhaps, she would have a shop of her own, and a spacious workshop where she could construct all manner of fascinating things.

But not yet.

With an inaudible sigh, Eleanora turned her attention away from her impractical dreams and back to the harp.

She did not like the clockwork mechanism that had been attached to the instrument in order for it to play alone. It was an ungainly, spiderlike contraption folded beneath the harp. When wound with the large brass key, dozens of thin metal appendages would deploy. Each one was tipped with a tiny hook to pluck the string, and their striking put Eleanora in mind of an army of scorpions, stinging the music to life.

It was strange that she should find the mechanics so unsettling, for normally she was fascinated by clockworks. But there was something about the underbody of the harp that she disliked, beyond all reason.

She was glad when Lady Thomas declared them finished, giving Eleanora leave to adjourn from the drawing room. And despite the fact that her mother brushed her fancies aside, Eleanora thought there was something unnatural about the harp.

AFTER MIDNIGHT, the Thomas's townhouse lay still and slumbering. Eleanora woke, her mouth dry. Moving by feel, she went to the table where the water pitcher stood, but when she lifted it, she could tell it was empty. Drat it.

There was nothing for it but go down to the kitchen and fetch herself a glass of water. Her mother might insist on ringing for a maid, but Eleanora did not want to wake a sleepy serving girl from her well-earned rest. Then there would be two of them unhappily awake in the middle of the night, instead of just one.

Eleanora drew on her oriental silk wrapper, conveniently hung over the foot of her bed, and felt about for her lambskin slippers. When she could only locate one, she slid to her bedside table. She did not like the stink of sulfur matches, but even more she did not relish the thought of the cold kitchen flagstones under her bare feet.

The match flared, stinging her eyes with light and fumes. She quickly lit the candle in its holder and blew the match out. Her wayward slipper peeked out from the far corner of the bed, and with a sigh she retrieved it, picked up the candle, and slipped out into the hallway.

The flame sent eerie shadows dancing over the walls,

and the air was cool and clammy. Drawing her wrapper closed with one hand, she hastened down the hall.

At the top of the staircase, she halted. Something was amiss. Holding her breath, she listened. Soft music drifted up from the drawing room.

Could one of the servants be awake, amusing themselves with playing?

It was a comforting notion, but the cold shiver along her spine told her otherwise. Especially as the plaintive notes were clearly the sound of a harp.

Pulse beating in the hollow of her throat, Eleanora crept down the stairs. She did not want to look into the drawing room—but she must. As she drew closer, she could almost make out the melody. Another step closer. Another.

The music stopped. Eleanora forced herself to hurry to the open door of the room. She lifted her candle, hoping to catch whoever was playing.

Moonlight shone in through the bow window, bathing the harp in silver and shadow. The room was empty, except for the shapes of the pianoforte and harpsichord, the guitar in its stand, and the mandolin hung upon the wall. No servant girl leapt up, stammering apologies. No restless denizen of the house was present at all.

Swallowing the acrid taste of fear, Eleanora went over to the harp. She could not bring herself to touch it, but bent to study the mechanism. How could it have played, with no one to wind it?

It was possible the clockwork had not fully unwound from the last time her mother had demonstrated the mechanical harp to her admiring friends. Yet Eleanora distinctly recalled the music coming to a normal conclusion, ending with a ringing chord and the applause of the listeners.

She shivered and backed away, unwilling to take her gaze from the harp. Reaching the doorway, she slipped behind the shelter of the wall and took a deep breath.

It was only a midnight fancy; some melody lodged in her head that she had imagined hearing. That was all.

Mouth dry as parchment, she went to the sink and poured herself a cup of water. Through the windows, she could see the gaslights from the main avenue shining fitfully through the hedges. Overhead, the lit form of an airship drifted high above the London streets, blurred by fog into an elongated moon.

Certainly the clockwork had malfunctioned. Sometime in the next few days she would have the opportunity to examine it. Lord Thomas was away at Parliament most afternoons, and Lady Thomas would no doubt have some small social engagement Eleanora could beg off attending.

Young ladies of Quality were not taught to sully their hands with manual labor, and certainly not with grease and gadgets. But Eleanora had always had a fascination for the mechanical. She'd dismantled any number of her toys when she was a child, trying to determine what animated her clockwork animals and steam-driven calliope.

Her nurse had discouraged her, and hidden the broken evidence from Viscount Thomas.

"But what makes them go?" Eleanora remembered

asking. "Have they a soul, like people do? Or are we clock-work inside, too?"

At that thought, she'd set her hand to her chest, wondering if she felt the whirring of gears or pumping of a steam engine. She had been told her heart resided beneath her ribs, but what, she wondered, powered it?

"They are just machines, and not for you to concern yourself over," Nurse had said, stuffing the remains of an eviscerated metal canary into the bottom of the rubbish bin. "Now, enough of this nonsense. If his lordship finds out, I'll be let go. And who will bury your toys then, miss?"

Eleanora had learned to keep her tinkering where her father could not see, but she had been delighted to find out there were people who studied such things.

"I would like to be an engineer," she'd announced at dinner one night, at the unfortunately innocent age of ten.

"What has that governess been teaching her?" Lord Thomas had said, setting his fork down with a clatter. "I'll have her removed immediately. Do endeavor to find her a more proper companion next time, Lady Thomas. If such a thing is within your capacity."

"Yes, dear," Lady Thomas had said, bending her head in acquiescence—but not before shooting Eleanora a look full of dire warning.

And so, sweetly indulgent Miss Tanager had been replaced by strict and stern Mrs. Corbin, and Eleanora closed her mouth, keeping her dreams and desires to herself.

For the next several years she'd comported herself like a lady—at least in public. At sixteen, she made her debut before the queen, and quickly learned how to make empty, convivial conversation at balls and parties.

In the last two years, however, she'd begun slipping out with only her maid in attendance and poking through the shops in the more questionable quarters of London. She loved the sooty, narrow streets where the clockmakers and steam engineers plied their trades, and the air was filled with whirring and buzzing and gouts of white, moist air.

It was there she had taken her pocket money and bought her first set of spanners. Later visits saw her returning home with gears and bits of bronze and copper wire concealed in her reticule. Her maid was loyal, and never said anything to Lord and Lady Thomas. Likely the woman knew she'd be summarily dismissed for not keeping Eleanora away from such places.

As if Eleanora would let anyone dissuade her from her passion.

The chill of the flagstones seeped through the soles of her slippers. She set her empty glass on the kitchen's wooden table and steadied herself for the journey back to her bedroom.

The downstairs remained silent except for the soft brush of her footsteps. She held her breath, her pulse accelerating as she approached the drawing room. Nothing stirred, no trickle of melody wended into the air. Still, the back of her neck prickled as she hurried past the open doorway. She did not feel safe until she had closed the door of her room behind her and turned the key, locking the door with a satisfactory thunk.

ELEANORA DID NOT HAVE a chance to tinker with the harp until four days later, when her mother went on an afternoon outing to bestow charity upon the orphans. Eleanora had stationed herself in the drawing room in case such an opportunity might arise.

"Are you quite certain you don't wish to accompany me?" Lady Thomas asked as she settled her cherry-decorated hat upon her upswept coiffure. "Lady Eldwin and her daughter will be coming, and it would do you good to cultivate their company."

"Perhaps next time," Eleanora said.

While they were acquainted, she'd never felt a particular resonance of fellowship with dark-haired Anne Eldwin. The girl had a dour disposition, her eyebrows always pinched together and a frown upon her mouth. Her younger sister, Belinda, had been much lighter of spirit— and fairer of coloring as well. The two sisters had been like night and day.

It was a tragedy that Belinda had drowned the summer before, in the lake near the Eldwin's country estate.

"Suit yourself," Lady Thomas said, with a sniff that indicated she would prefer it if Eleanora did no such thing, but instead bent to her mother's wishes.

"I shall be glad to remain at home." Eleanora gave her mother an unruffled smile. "Pay my regards to the Eldwins."

She continued sketching the pot of narcissus on the drawing room side table, pretending to be wholly engaged until her mother at last took her leave. Still, Eleanora scribed the trumpet-like shape of the flowers on the page until she heard the steam-carriage pull away, the iron-bound wheels rumbling over the cobbles.

She flipped the page of her sketch book, turning to the study she had made of the clockwork harp. It would come in handy, particularly if she dismantled any part of the instrument. Mother would not be pleased if her new instrument were broken.

Eleanora set her book down and pulled the spanner set from behind the divan's cushions, where she had earlier concealed it.

Despite her outward serenity, nervous energy ran just beneath her skin as she knelt before the harp. Carefully, she wound the key, then sat back as the spidery legs deployed and played a lively rendition of a Bach minuet.

The piece ended, the mechanism folded closed, and the harp was still once again.

Eleanora waited a full five minutes, but nothing further happened. Very well. She unrolled the canvas sheltering the set of tools and chose her second smallest wrench. She was not entirely certain about how to begin, but she felt more secure as her fingers wrapped around the solid metal.

Carefully, she rotated the harp so the back of the soundbox faced the window. Intermittent sun shone in, enough to illuminate the hollow inside of the harp through the oval holes set along the length of the instrument. The plucking mechanism was fastened to the outside of the box, but the gears that powered it were located inside. That must be where her answers lay.

Eleanora peered into the soundbox through one of the holes. The clockwork seemed perfectly fine at first glance. Held above the mechanism were a half dozen articulated arms, each one holding a thin metallic sheet with holes and bumps punched into the metal. Those must be the scores of the melodies the harp played, the pattern directing how the outer mechanism should strike the strings, like one would find inside a player piano.

Something glimmered at the bottom of the soundbox, something that resembled silk rather than metal or wood.

Frowning, she set her spanner down and rolled back the puffy sleeve of her gown. She did not relish the idea of reaching into the innards of the harp, but it was not as though the mechanism would bite. Clockwork could not hurt her.

She hoped.

With a deep breath to steady herself, she inserted her arm into the bottom hole of the soundbox. She could not see what she was doing, but let her fingertips glide over the teeth of the gears, then further down. She managed to fit her arm in just past the elbow, and continued to grope about.

At last her questing touch met a tangled softness. Her hand jerked away involuntarily at the impression she'd encountered a spider's nest, or something equally nasty. Gritting her teeth, she forced her fingers to close about the unsettling material.

She drew it out, her arm prickling as though some multi-legged creature were about to leap up and run along her skin. The instant her hand was clear of the harp, she dropped the object on the multi-colored carpet and rubbed vigorously at her forearm and fingers, trying to erase the sensation.

What lay on the carpet was not a creature of any kind. Eleanor leaned over to inspect it, still wary of touching the thing. It was a necklace woven out of golden fibers. An ornate braided flower in the center was decorated with a few pearls. The leafy fringe at the bottom was what she had first touched.

Gingerly, she poked at it. When the necklace did not move, she picked it up and studied it closely. It was, if she were not mistaken, woven of human hair.

Memorial jewelry made of the deceased's hair was quite fashionable, although why the necklace had been hidden in the bottom of the harp was a mystery. Even more disturbing: who was the dead woman whose hair made up the necklace?

"I don't believe in ghosts," Eleanora announced to the empty drawing room. "Particularly not ones who take up residence inside clockworks. The two are mutually exclusive."

Despite the firmness of her voice, however, she felt rather disquieted.

She tucked the necklace into the pocket of her morning gown. Perhaps with its removal, the harp would cease its uncanny playing. If it had ever actually done so, and the music had not been simply a figment of her imagination.

Briskly, she turned the harp back around. It seemed

her spanners would not be needed, and she must put them away before her mother returned. She slipped her small wrench back into its pocket and re-rolled the canvas.

As she ascended the stairs, she heard the steam-powered carriage puffing and clattering up the street, bearing Lady Thomas home. Eleanora paused and glanced out the stairwell window, but it appeared the Eldwin ladies were no longer accompanying her mother.

Eleanora tucked her tools into their hiding place at the bottom of her wardrobe, along with the necklace, and met her mother in the front hallway.

"How were the orphans?" she asked.

"Ungrateful." Lady Thomas sniffed and pulled off her kid gloves. "You ought to have come."

"I will, when you next visit them," Eleanora said. "Shall we ring for tea in the drawing room?"

Lady Thomas did enjoy her civilized comforts. It would be no use questioning her until she was sufficiently recovered from her outing.

"That would be lovely. I need something to calm my nerves."

Some minutes later, the two of them sat on the davenport, the second-best silver tea service set on the table before them. Lady Thomas nodded to the maid when she brought a plate of biscuits, then poured out two cups of tea.

Eleanor stirred a lump of sugar into hers, then waited until her mother took a sip from the gold-rimmed cup and let out a sigh.

"I was wondering," Eleanora said. "Where exactly did you find the clockwork harp?"

At the time, she'd assumed her mother had purchased it from one of the instrument dealers she was fond of frequenting. In addition to the larger instruments in the drawing room, there were several flutes made of metal, wood, and bone, a mechanical snare drum (never used), and an antique lyre.

"It's quite the showpiece, I do agree," Lady Thomas said, glancing at the harp. "You know, I snatched it out from beneath Lady Eldwin's nose."

"Did you?" Eleanora set her teacup down.

Lady Thomas gave her a smug nod. "I was on High Street, and a steam omnibus had broken down, blocking traffic. A tinker in the most colorful cart was stopped there, and I saw the harp in the back. Of course, I immediately recognized it was a treasure."

"Of course."

"I asked the fellow if he would sell it to me, and he replied he was charged with delivering it to Lady Eldwin. I told him I would pay him double the commission. It did not take long for him to accept my coin, and move the harp into my carriage."

"Wasn't Lady Elwin upset?" Eleanora asked.

"She claims she knows nothing of any such instrument. Hmph. Clearly she was jealous of my coup, and did not want to admit it."

Eleanora gave the harp a long, considering look. If the instrument were somehow connected to the Eldwin family, then it was entirely possible the necklace she had removed from it was made of dead Belinda Eldwin's hair.

Why, then, did the family not know of the harp?

"Did the tinker say who had built the instrument?" she asked.

Lady Thomas waved her hand. "That minstrel mechanist in Suffolk. He's rather well known, although the name escapes me at the moment."

"Tallesin," Eleanora supplied.

Indeed, if the harp had been built in his workshop, her mother had taken possession of a quite valuable instrument. Eleanora hoped it had not cost them too dearly.

She could not fault the workmanship; the ivory and pearl inlays on the top of the soundbox were exquisite, and the tone of the harp was sweet and true. It was only that the clockwork did not match the harp, and it perplexed her. Especially if it had come from the master minstrel's workshop.

"Yes, that's the name." Lady Thomas took another sip of tea.

"Isn't the Eldwin's summer estate in Suffolk?"

"Indeed. Which is why I believe Lady Eldwin is telling me untruths. I might have taken pity on her, had she actually confessed to commissioning the harp, but as it is..." Lady Thomas lifted her shoulders in a delicate shrug.

The maneuverings for position among the top ladies of the gentry generally were of little interest to Eleanora, but she suspected that her mother was incorrect in this matter.

"Speaking of the Eldwins, I trust your gown is in

working order?" Lady Thomas asked. "The ball is in two days, after all."

"I will try it on now, but I'm certain the lifter mechanisms are well-tuned."

If they were not, she would simply tweak the lifters until her skirts floated about her like a cloud. It was an interesting fashion, and Eleanora did take some satisfaction in wearing something that was half contraption and half ball gown.

It was not until she was upstairs, with her wardrobe open, that she realized the harp had not made a single sound while they discussed its provenance, and the Eldwins. She glanced down at the drawer holding the necklace. If she returned it to its hiding place, would the harp begin its mysterious sighing once more?

She did not want to find out. Carefully removing her mechanized ball gown from the cedar-lined wardrobe, she closed the door, leaving the necklace and its secrets in darkness.

THAT NIGHT, Eleanora woke at the brush of a cold hand over her forehead. Heart pounding, she opened her eyes wide, searching the quiet shadows of her bedroom.

"Who's there?" she whispered.

No one answered, but the door of her bedroom swung open. Almost, she saw a ghostly figure of a girl in a long white dress outlined in the doorway. Eleanora rubbed her eyes. The vision was a product of dreaming, surely.

It took her several moments to gather her courage and slip out of bed to close the door. The wool rug was scratchy against her bare toes. She set her hand to the knob, then paused.

Faint music drifted down the hallway.

Curiosity warred with fear, and won. She snatched her wrapper and hastily donned her slippers, then went to the end of the hall. As she had known it would, the sound of a harp emanated from the drawing room.

The melody was plaintive and slow, and after a few bars more, she recognized it as *Greensleeves*. Was that tune inscribed upon one of the metal cards inside the harp, or did ghostly fingers pull it forth from the harp?

Quietly, she descended the stairs. When she reached the bottom, the melody changed. It was another old ballad, and Eleanora hummed under her breath, trying to identify the refrain. *By the bonny mill-dams of Binoorie.*

A chill swept over her.

The harp was playing *The Cruel Sister*, a ballad recounting how a sister murdered her younger sibling by drowning.

"No," Eleanora whispered.

She did not want to know this. Belinda Eldwin's death was accidental. Surely her sister Anne had not pushed her into the lake.

Yet the image came to her of fair Belinda, her skirts dragging her down into the cold waters while she held out her hand to her sister, pleading for rescue.

Oh, why hadn't Lady Thomas left well enough alone! The harp intended to haunt the Eldwins had instead come to the wrong house. And Eleanora was even more convinced that Lady Eldwin was innocent of all knowledge of the cursed instrument.

A shiver wracked Eleanora while the notes of the ballad softly filled the air.

Why had Tallesin had fashioned the harp in the first place?

Perhaps the answer lay within the old ballad. Lord Thomas's library was well stocked, and she knew where the collections of folklore and ballads were shelved.

Unfortunately, she would have to pass the drawing room to reach the library.

Clutching her wrapper tightly closed, she crept down the wide hallway. Fear clogged her throat, but as soon as she reached the open drawing room door, the music stopped.

Eleanora forced herself to look in. There was no moon, just fog outside the bow window. The harp stood alone, each string faintly outlined in a pale glimmer.

She had to swallow twice before she could speak.

"I will try to help you," she said, softly. Though she did not know how she would accomplish it.

There was no acknowledgement, no chord of thanks or ghostly form materializing to make her a bow. The light faded from the harp, until it was a shadow silhouetted against the gray fog.

Slowly, Eleanora's heartbeat returned to normal. She took a deep breath, then continued on to the library.

Banked coals in the fireplace glowed red. She lifted one of the mantelpiece candles and bent to light it from the coals, welcoming the heat against her hands and face. The wick flared to life, and she squinted against the sudden brightness.

A few minutes' searching yielded up the thick tome titled *Collected Ballads of Scotland and the North*. The gold lettering on the cover gleamed in the candle light. Eleanora paged through until she found what she was seeking: *The Cruel Sister*. She skimmed the text, fingers growing colder as she read.

She had remembered it correctly; the ballad recounted the tale of two sisters, one fair, one dark. A knight came to court the eldest, but instead fell in love with the younger sister. Consumed with jealousy, the dark girl threw her sister into the sea and refused to help her as she drowned. All of that was terrible enough, but the end of the ballad made Eleanora's heart freeze.

> A minstrel walked along the strand,
> And saw the maiden float to land.
> He made a harp of her breastbone,
> Whose sound would melt a heart of stone.

That would explain Tallesin's involvement, though why he would build a harp out of a dead girl's body, she could not fathom. In truth, the instrument was mostly made of wood. But the ivory inlays took on new meaning. She shuddered, and continued reading.

> He took three locks of her yellow hair,
> And with them strung the harp so rare.

The harp was not strung with hair, but with sinew. Eleanora most emphatically did *not* want to think about where it had come from. The hair necklace hidden inside the soundbox fulfilled that role well enough.

Hair, and bone, and sinew. It explained why removing the necklace had not kept the harp from playing. There was enough of Belinda Eldwin in the instrument to anchor her ghost.

> He took it to her father's hall
> To play the harp before them all.
> But when he placed it on the stone
> The harp began to play alone.

And that was where the plan had gone awry. The harp was not in the dead girl's home—though it certainly played alone.

The ballad went on to describe how the harp sang of the girl's murder, and, in tears, the elder sister confessed.

Well then.

Eleanora closed the book and stared absently at the flickering candle flame. It was clear she must convince Lady Thomas to take the harp to Anne Eldwin's betrothal ball. Appearances meant everything to her mother. Lady Thomas was proud and possessive, but she could be talked into showing her generosity of spirit by giving Anne Eldwin the harp as a wedding gift.

And once there, Eleanora only hoped the harp would perform as described.

THE ELDWIN'S ballroom shone brightly, illuminated by crystal-bedecked gaslight chandeliers hanging from the tall ceiling. Light glittered off gemstones fastened about throats and arms—rubies and diamonds, emeralds and sapphires, sending glints of color over the gaily-dressed throng.

The air was sweet with mingled perfumes as Eleanora followed her mother across the polished marble floor to where the Eldwins stood on a dais, greeting their guests. The skirts of her gown billowed and floated about her like a gossamer cloud, the lifter mechanism expanding into empty space and pulling back when she got too near any object.

Behind them, a footman carried the harp, draped in a blue silk cloth. Eleanora bit her lip, her heart sinking. What if she had been wrong? Haunted midnight melodies now seemed the product of her own fevered imagination.

The noisy, well-lit ballroom was a bastion of normalcy. Even if there were a ghost, she would not materialize in such a place.

"My dear Lady Eldwin, Lord Eldwin," Eleanora's mother said as they arrived at the foot of the dais. "Our most sincere congratulations to your daughter, Anne, upon her betrothal."

Dark-haired Anne, standing beside her mother, nodded, her face unsmiling. At her other side, her betrothed, Sir William Hunt, looked a bit glum as well.

Lady Eldwin inclined her head in thanks. "I see you have brought us a gift. How kind."

"Yes." Lady Thomas gave her an insincere smile. "I thought it only right, in the spirit of friendship, to bestow this fine instrument upon Miss Anne."

She beckoned to the footman, who set the harp down on the marble floor and pulled the silk cloth off with a flourish. Eleanora watched closely, but none of the Eldwins showed any flash of recognition—or fear—at the sight.

"How very cunning," Anne Eldwin said. "Does it play?"

"Of course it plays." Lady Thomas sniffed, then looked at Eleanora. "Do wind it, my dear."

Heart thumping, Eleanora bent and turned the brass key three times around.

Nothing happened.

The Eldwins' looks of expectation turned to boredom.

"Play," Eleanora whispered, turning the key again.

One of the spidery legs jerked, then fell off, landing on the marble with a metallic ping. Some of the nearby guests laughed.

"A pity it's not in working order," Lady Eldwin said. "I suppose it can go in the back parlor as a curiosity." She turned her gaze to the next guests in line, clearly dismissing Lady Thomas and her gift.

"Wait!" Eleanora cried.

Impulsively, she pulled one of her hairpins free. She scooped up the leg and deftly re-attached it, bending her hairpin to help hold the appendage in place.

The clockwork instantly sprung into motion, plucking

out a sweet waltz. From the corner of her eye, Eleanora saw a tall, white-haired gentleman push through the crowd. He stared at the harp with a look comprised equally of relief and revulsion.

The waltz slowed, and as it did, the lights began to dim. Lord Eldwin commenced chiding his wife about not taking proper care of the chandeliers, but he fell silent as a chilly blast of air swept through the ballroom. The mechanism folded itself beneath the soundbox of the harp, yet the instrument continued to play. *The Cruel Sister* rang out, and Anne Eldwin's sallow skin turned pale.

The lyrics of the ballad echoed in Eleanora's mind.

> The first string sang a doleful sound:
> "The bride her younger sister drowned."

Whispers of consternation rose from the assembled guests, all attention drawn to the front of the dais. The harp was beginning to glow, bluish-white light outlining the strings and pouring from the soundbox, where Eleanora had replaced the hair necklace.

Lady Eldwin took a step back, her eyes wide, but her daughter seemed frozen in place. A single tear slipped down her cheek. Then another. Beside the harp, a figure coalesced—a young woman with long, flowing hair, gowned in white. Slowly, she raised her hand and pointed at Anne Eldwin.

"No!" Anne cried, her voice filled with terror. Tears glazed her face.

Beside her, Sir William Hunt stared at the ghost, love and longing clear in his expression.

"Belinda," he whispered.

The glowing figure nodded, once. A cold wind whipped about the ballroom, jangling the crystals on the dim chandeliers and blowing skirts wildly about.

Quickly, Eleanora deactivated the mechanical lifters of her gown to keep it from twisting and billowing. The white-haired gentleman moved to stand beside her, his gaze fixed on the ghost.

"She will have her vengeance at last," he murmured.

The wind died down to an icy breath, and quiet filled the emptiness it left behind. The ghost of Belinda Eldwin glided toward her sister, until they stood face to face. Mirrored dark and light, alive and dead.

Slowly, the dead girl raised her hand and pointed at her sister.

"I pushed her in," Anne Eldwin sobbed. "Belinda—oh, I am so sorry!"

For still moment, the ghost of Belinda Eldwin regarded her murderer. Then, with a sigh, the glowing figure walked right through the living flesh of her elder sister.

Anne let out a harrowing shriek and fell to the floor. Sir William went to one knee beside his betrothed and took her wrist.

"She has fainted," he said after a moment. "Someone, fetch smelling salts."

Eleanora noted that he let go of the young lady's wrist rather quickly and wiped his fingers on his trousers, his expression veering into loathing.

As the lights brightened, Lady Elwin regarded the harp, her face twisted with despair.

"Take it away!" she cried, then turned, weeping, into her husband's shoulder.

Conversations sprang up all over the ballroom, loud and speculative. Eleanora felt overcome with sadness. Justice had been served, surely, but she had not enjoyed her part in it.

"Who are you, sir?" she asked, catching the arm of the white-haired gentleman.

"My name is Tallesin Woodweft," he said.

"But... you are the minstrel mechanic who made the harp." Eleanora studied his lined face, his faded blue eyes.

"Indeed, to my sorrow. A sad tale, that."

"Perhaps you might tell me. Some time, under better circumstances."

He nodded and handed her his card. "You seem a sensible young lady. Do write—I feel we might have a beneficial future correspondence."

"I shall." She tucked the card into her reticule.

With a weary nod, he turned and beckoned to one of the nearby footmen.

"I shall remove this cursed harp," the minstrel said. "Convey it to my carriage."

The footman hesitated, then, at an impatient gesture from Tallesin Woodweft, lifted the instrument. As he hefted it into his arms, the clockwork structure disengaged from the base of the harp and fell to the marble floor with a metallic clatter. The footman started violently and dropped the instrument.

"No," Tallesin cried, lunging forward as Eleanora rushed to help.

Too late. The harp shattered, bits of wood flying. The strings snapped from the soundbox in a cacophony of discord, and in that sound, Eleanora heard the last cry of an unearthly voice.

The noise silenced the guests again, and they moved back from the ruined harp lying in the middle of the ballroom.

The music was done, the ballad sung, and the onlookers left to pick up the pieces: cracked wood and tangled strings, splintered inlay, and the pale weave of a dead girl's hair.

∿

MUSIC'S PRICE

Although this story is also in my Tales of Feyland & Faerie *collection, it is so intrinsically about magic and music that I had to include it here as well. The original publication of Music's Price can be found in* Fiction River: Hex in the City *edited by Kerrie Hughes, along with stories by Seanan McGuire and other fabulous urban fantasy authors.*

SOMETIMES, WHEN JEREMY CAHILL PRACTICED THE CELLO, he'd glimpse *things* out of the corner of his eye. Oddly-joined creatures scuttling along the dingy baseboard of their midtown Manhattan apartment, shimmers of brightness in the dark hallway where no stray sunbeam ever reached.

He was eight the first time he saw them, and tried to tell Ma, but she'd laughed and tousled his hair.

"Ah, Jemmy, you have the Irish gift of blarney. Your

gran would be proud. Now, put the instrument away and help me with supper."

As his skill on the cello grew, the uncanny visitors came more frequently. Twig-jointed creatures gathered like bare branches outside the window to listen, slight maidens in gossamer-pale gowns danced like moonbeams—one moment shadow, the next a flicker of light. No one else could see them, and the instant he stopped playing, they vanished.

The creatures were uncanny, but not frightening. Until the day a hollow-eyed banshee appeared, dipping a boy's clothes in the sudden, blood-red stream cutting through his bedroom.

The next morning, his cousin was hit by a car while riding his bike to school, and died instantly. After that, Jeremy refused to practice, refused to even take his cello out of the case, a case that now resembled a coffin.

His dad called him into the living room after a month of sullen non-practicing.

"All the money we've spent over the years, for nothing?" Dad's face reddened, anger thickening his brogue.

He paced around his tan recliner, yelling about the cost, the waste, the brilliance that already had a teacher from the renowned Juilliard School of Music giving Jeremy twice-a-month special lessons.

"Well?" he finally demanded, meaty arms crossed. "Give me one reason."

Jeremy stared at the green carpeting, sick guilt sticking in his throat. He shook his head.

"Jaysus." Dad let out a beer-scented gust of breath. "Get

your coat, lad. Maybe your gran can make some sense of you. Don't come home until she does. And you're ready to practice the damned cello again."

It was a slow bus ride uptown. Jeremy stared out the sleet-spattered windows the whole time, ignoring the other passengers.

When he showed up at her door, Gran took one look at Jeremy's face and sat him down at her kitchen table. She poured him out a cup of strong black tea, using the good china with the gold rim. Without a word, she pushed the sugar and milk over, then waited quietly while he drank. It was the taste of safety.

Surrounded by the yellow warmth of her kitchen, the misery inside him finally uncoiled. He was thirteen, too old to cry, but he set his forehead on the table and wept like a little kid. The lace tablecloth pressed uncomfortably into his skin, but that was nothing compared to the shattering of his heart.

"There, there, *mo chroi*," Gran said, rubbing his hunched-over shoulders. "Tell me."

Her steel-grey hair was crimped in perfect waves, her dress—he'd never seen her in pants—printed with saggy blue flowers. She clomped around the kitchen in her thick black shoes, fixing a plate of sandwiches.

In between blowing his nose, and more tea, and devouring the sandwiches slathered with butter, he told her.

She nodded wisely. "Tis the Sight, love. A rare gift, to be able to see the fair folk."

"I don't want it." He was weird enough, being the

musical genius kid, but this—just, no. "I can't play Gran. It's not fair. I can't play ever again unless it goes away."

His voice cracked on the words. Music was the air he breathed—the thing that carried him through the bitter halls of Taft Junior High, the shell protecting his soft, inner core. He couldn't *not* play. But he couldn't bear what the music brought.

Gran studied him, her thin lips pursed. "Well now. Bide here a moment."

She stumped into the parlor, and he heard her opening drawers and rustling around. When she returned, she laid an odd assortment on the table in front of him: a small square of linen, a spool of red thread, a four-leaf clover leached to gray from decades of being pressed in her Bible, and a hard, dry berry the color of old blood.

Jeremy stared at the objects, trying to guess their use. They made no pattern he could see, especially when his grandmother added the tin of oatmeal and her prized crystal salt cellar.

"Um, Gran. What are you doing?"

It looked like a crazy recipe—one he had no intention of tasting. She sat across from him, the spindle-backed chair creaking when she leaned forward.

"You need a charm, my lad. A ward to banish the fair folk, to keep your own heart from breaking. I see how it is with you. Open this." She handed him the smooth yellow tin.

He pried the top off, and she took a pinch of oats and dropped them in the center of the linen square.

"Wait, what? Is this some kind of magic spell or something?" Jeremy frowned, feeling his lips squeeze together. "That's crazy."

Gran gave him a stern look. "This, from the boy that sees the fair folk. Come now, Jemmy. Give me the rowan berry."

That must be the dried bead of fruit. One by one he handed his grandmother each item she requested. She carefully placed them on the cloth, humming softly. At the end, she picked up her salt cellar and gave the entire concoction a thorough salting. Grains of salt drifted over the table like snow.

"Thread the needle, there's a good lad. Double-strung." She folded the edges of the linen square together.

Jeremy licked the end of the thread and managed to get it through the eye on the second try. Gran nodded at him and deftly began sewing precise red stitches against the white cloth, making a neat little packet. Her humming turned to words, the crush and wash of Gaelic like waves on a distant island shore, soughing and sighing up against stone.

When she finished, she tied a firm knot at the end and snipped the thread with a small pair of scissors.

"Some string now," she said. "Fetch it from the top drawer, there."

Jeremy pulled the drawer open and studied the jumble inside. The catchall, the one place in Gran's kitchen that wasn't perfectly tidy and neat. A long curl of one of his old cello strings sprung up to tangle his fingers. Boy, Gran sure kept some useless bits around.

"Bring that," she said.

"My old *D*? What for?"

"It's string, isn't it?" She gave him a level look.

No point in arguing, though technically it was made of nylon and steel, not string at all. Still, he wouldn't argue with Gran—not when she put the eye on him like that. He handed the string to her and she affixed the linen packet halfway down with loops of red thread. Murmuring in Gaelic again, she took the needle and stabbed her index finger.

"Gran!"

"Hush now, *acushla*." A fat, bright drop of blood fell to the center of the linen, spread and wicked into the cloth, a crimson starburst. She held up the weird-looking necklace, the ends of the *D* string corkscrewing around her fingers. "Your charm of safekeeping. Wear it when you play, and the fair folk will stay their distance."

He took it, weighing it in his palm. The doubt must have shown on his face, because she cupped her wrinkled hands around his.

"I promise," she said.

"Okay." He tucked the charm in his pocket. "Thanks, Gran. I should go home."

She firmed her lips. "Believe."

"I will."

He'd try, anyway. And she was right; he'd seen way more strange things than he could explain. Maybe the charm would help save him. Jeremy kissed her dry, rose-scented cheek, and, hope catching in his throat, caught the bus back midtown.

When he got home, he didn't say anything to his dad, just got his cello out, tuned it up, and started practicing.

Gran's charm worked. At least, it did for the next seven years.

INSIDE THE CHURCH, the dimly-lit air swirled with candle smoke and incense. After the priest finished saying the words he nodded to where Jeremy sat, to the left of Gran's black coffin. Jeremy pulled his cello back against his body, the wood gleaming like rich toffee. The long scratch marring the finish was hidden by his black trouser leg—a small mercy in a day filled with too much misery.

He glanced at his parents sitting in the front pew, their hands tightly woven together. Dad was thinner now, his skin grayish from the chemo. He'd removed his ever-present cap, and the bare skin of his scalp shone with perspiration. Beside him, Jeremy's mother looked smaller, the strain of the last year etched on her face in new lines.

The priest cleared his throat, and Jeremy began to play. He started with one of Gran's favorites, *Si Bheag, Si Mhor*, the notes rising up to flutter like moths against the stained glass.

On the daylit side of the windows, he glimpsed twiggy creatures crouching. A distant siren sped through the city streets, and he heard the echo of his name in its high wailing.

No. Oh no.

The fair folk had returned. They couldn't enter the church, but he felt them outside. Waiting.

Fear thick in his throat, Jeremy kept playing. He'd promised Gran he'd play at her funeral.

"Not just the sad tunes, Jemmy," she'd told him, her fingers frail in his grasp, her skin yellow against the too-white hospital pillows. "You must remember the good, as well. Play a reel for me. The angels will like that."

She'd looked at him, the echo of her old self brightening in her eyes.

Don't go, Gran. Grief had crushed his breath, but he'd managed a smile for her.

"I will," he said.

But he'd never expected the cost. As the music spooled out from under his fingers, the charm that had held the fair folk at bay for so long faltered, its power fading. Still, he played.

Jeremy's dad frowned, his way of holding back tears, and Jeremy slid into a different tune, *The Broken Pledge*, an old reel in a minor key. For Gran's memory, for the scrap of linen and string tucked beneath his shirt—useless now.

He played the tune three times through, then lifted his bow from the strings, the cello still vibrating against his knees.

Nobody applauded—they wouldn't at a funeral—but he could see how the power of the music touched them. His mother blew her nose discreetly into her linen kerchief. The priest gave a final blessing, and freed the congregation. The burial was later that afternoon.

Jeremy waited for the church to empty, fear and sorrow

curdling in his stomach. He didn't want to set foot outside those consecrated walls. Didn't want to say goodbye to Gran, and the magic that had protected him for so long.

"Lovely playing," his mother said, clutching her handkerchief. "I'm so sorry about…. Well. Your gran would be proud."

His dad gripped his shoulder, with a hand that still had some strength to it.

"Well done," he said, a gruff edge in his voice—pride and guilt tangled together.

It wasn't Dad's fault he'd gotten sick and the money had run out like water through a sieve. The scholarship Jeremy got from Juilliard wasn't enough to bridge the sudden, yawning chasm in his family's finances. The only option was to drop out of music school. They called it a "leave of absence," but Jeremy knew he wouldn't be back. Not unless things changed drastically—which wasn't going to happen.

The back of his neck tightened as he trailed his parents out of the church. He couldn't see the fair folk, but he sensed their presence. Watching him.

When Gran was buried and the last words said, Jeremy took the subway back to his apartment. He stuck his cello case in the corner, facing away from him. There was no reason to play—no teachers demanding concertos, no quartets depending on him—and every reason not to.

What if, the next time he played, the banshee came again, warning of his dad's imminent death? No. He wouldn't bear that guilt. To keep the fair folk at bay, he'd stop playing, though his soul might bleed dry from it.

Jeremy ignored his cello for three weeks, spent his days

handing in job applications everywhere. But apparently a Juilliard drop-out wasn't even qualified to wash dishes at the deli down the street. The smell of their pastrami sandwiches made his mouth water—he'd been living on ramen and canned peaches for a week—but he couldn't afford anything more. He left, the doorbell jangling behind him. The winter wind slapped his cheeks, but colder still was the knowledge he'd run out of choices.

Pulling his wool pea coat tight, Jeremy trudged back to his unheated apartment. The tiny studio would no longer be his if he didn't come up with rent within the next three days.

He could sell his cello—but the thought made his stomach churn. No. Gran had helped pay for it. Besides, he couldn't get what the instrument was worth on such short notice, and he refused to pawn it.

Hands cold, trying not to dwell on what he was doing, he slung his cello over his shoulder and headed to the West Avenue subway station.

After he'd left school, he'd made a decent enough living —all right, a scraping-by—playing for tips in the subway. He'd found a perfect corner to busk in; close enough to the heater vents so his fingers didn't stiffen from the cold, and enough out of the way that nobody tripped over his cello as they rushed by.

The station was grimed and oily, the tiled walls smeared with handprints, the concrete saturated with acres of ground-in dirt. Bright fluorescent lights cast jagged shadows over the station sign; WEST AVENUE printed in stark black letters.

A hollow wind whooshed from the train tunnel, stirring the discarded gum wrappers and paper cups that had collected in Jeremy's corner. At least nobody had taken the spot. He scooted the trash out of the way with the side of his shoe, then set up his folding stool and unpacked his cello. The battered fedora on his head had a five-dollar bill glued inside. He'd almost ripped it out to buy that pastrami sandwich, but seed-money was crucial—a cue that people should throw real money into his hat, not just dimes and pennies.

He tethered the fedora to his shoelace with a strand of fishing line. When he'd first started busking, he'd learned the hard way how impossible it was to chase a thief while carrying a naked cello. He'd lost nearly thirty bucks that day. Even worse, he'd put a long, painful scrape down his cello's side.

The rumble of the approaching train set his strings to vibrating.

Jeremy took a deep breath and tuned up. Nothing happened, and the tight knot under his ribs eased. Maybe Gran's funeral service had been a fluke. Maybe he was still safe. He lifted one hand to his chest and pressed the charm through the cloth of his t-shirt; the stained linen still strung on a tarnished D around his neck.

With a screech, the train pulled to a stop and the doors hissed open. He pulled his bow across the strings, letting the sweet precision of a Bach sonata soar into the echoing space before it filled up with the clack of shoes, the blur of conversation.

The crowd thickened, streaming past. He'd gotten there

just before the commuter hour, the best time to busk. Jeremy didn't openly look at his hat. Another lesson learned. Even though money was the whole point, it was bad form for the performer to pay attention to his take, at least where people could see. They preferred the illusion that musicians played only for love.

Still, watching from the corner of his eye, it looked like *nothing* was going into his hat. No bright flash of coins, no flutter of bills. He switched to a faster movement of the Bach.

When the last passengers trailed past, Jeremy pulled the hat over. It held the three quarters and five-spot he'd salted the hat with—and nothing else. Not even a dime.

"Oh, come on," he said to the empty station.

He'd always gotten *something* when he played—a few bucks at least, some pennies. This wasn't just unfair, it was wrong in a way that set his teeth on edge.

For the next wave of commuters, he played Brahms, then Saint-Saens. Nothing.

Anger warmed him through.

"I know what you're doing," he said to the shadows lurking at the edge of the tunnel.

He almost, almost, packed up his cello. But he couldn't leave the station with pockets as empty as he'd come in.

The train whooshed up, disgorging people. Jeremy played Bartok, Bloch, the most modern pieces he knew. His hat stayed empty. Rush hour was almost over, and his chance of making any worthwhile money slipping away.

Curses on them.

He was finally there, playing, and it wasn't enough.

Fingers tight around his bow, Jeremy waited until the crowd was upon him. Then he launched into Gran's favorite jig; *The Lark in the Morning.*

Beyond the emptying platform, the shadows crept closer on spindle-shanks and goblin feet. He swallowed, hard, and kept playing. Eyes watched him from the edges. Things moved where they shouldn't.

But his hat filled with uncanny speed.

As the station emptied, Jeremy stilled his cello strings. He pulled his hat over, and caught his breath. Money filled the battered fedora. Carefully smoothing each bill, he counted his take. Forty-two dollars and seventy-three cents.

So, that's how it was going to be. Play the old tunes, or end up homeless on the bitter winter streets.

"Fine," he said, though it was so far from fine he wanted to weep.

One more wave of commuters left. If he was going to do this, he'd do it all the way. Just once.

This time he played from his heart, the way he hadn't let himself before. The sweet notes unfurled from beneath his fingers, the body of his cello resonating against his chest as he played one of his best tunes; *Farewell to Ireland.* The crowd flowed past, fingers drumming in time against legs, against briefcases. One lady held her phone out toward him for a moment before moving on. Though nobody lingered—they almost never did—it took longer than usual for the station to clear.

When the last set of heels disappeared up the stairs, Jeremy looked in his hat. Blinked, heartbeat pounding in his throat. The fedora was overflowing with bills, and not just singles.

"Damn," he breathed.

He counted the money out into a neat stack. One-hundred-sixty-five dollars and twenty-two cents. Unbelievable.

An unearthly giggle from the far platform, the glitter of a fey eye—it was past time for him to leave. Shivering, Jeremy shoved the money in his pocket and jammed his fedora on his head.

He closed his cello case, snicking the latches shut. The sound echoed, louder than it should, and a chill clutched the back of his neck. Something was watching from deep in the subway tunnel. A murmur built, like the sound of untamed waves. Keeping his gaze averted, Jeremy shouldered his cello and dashed up the stairs into the neon-broken night above.

But the next afternoon he reluctantly hauled his cello back to the grubby corner of the West Avenue Station. He was still short on the rent, though another few hours' playing should do it. Then he could stop; for good.

What if he didn't stop?

He tried to push the thought to the back of his mind, but it kept surfacing. The possibilities froze him with terror, burned him with hope.

If he played another day or two, gritted his teeth and tried not to see the creatures the music brought, he could make enough to help with Dad's next treatment. The fair folk already haunted his nightmares, after all. He could bear it a little longer.

Maybe.

Jeremy rosined his bow, the faint scent of old sap tickling his nose as he pulled the horsehair back and forth across the dark rectangle of rosin. Even before he started playing, he glimpsed them lurking in the shadows—misshapen bodies and legs that bent the wrong way, the starlit sheen of wings.

"I don't believe in you," he told them. The lie grated in his throat.

He waited to play until the trains disgorged their passengers, and stopped his music the instant the last person passed. Then began again at the next wave of commuters. Jaw tight, he played the hardest tunes he knew: complex five part slip-jigs, rambunctious reels pulsing in duple-beat rhythms, polkas that ratcheted his bow from string to string.

The fair folk watched. And listened. And came closer, their numbers growing.

Tens, twenties poured into his hat. Even a fifty, from a man who wore a suit worth ten times that amount. Jeremy didn't feel too guilty. People only put in what they could spare. A single bill, multiplied by a few hundred, added up.

He went home with over a thousand dollars, aching shoulders—and an unearthly escort. A chime of fey laughter in a dark alleyway, something flitting between parked cars, a black dog trotting down the sidewalk half a block behind, tongue lolling.

Jeremy whirled. "Leave me alone!"

Just another crazy yelling on the Manhattan streets. Nobody even looked his way.

Bitter knowledge sifted through his body, speeding his heart, drying his mouth. In all the old stories Gran had told him, there was no escape from the fair folk.

Not when they wanted you.

THE NEXT DAY, Jeremy paused at the top of the West Avenue Station stairs. Cello case straps digging into his shoulders, he tilted his face up to the wan winter sun, trying to memorize the feeling of sunlight against his skin.

Chill fingers combed through his hair, icy wind-borne maidens invisible to the passers-by on the street. Creatures leaned out from the bare-twigged bushes to clutch at his jeans with long, crooked nails.

Jemmy Cahill. The syllables of his name in the squeal of brakes, the cries of children, the sudden thrum of pigeon wings as a flock arose from the stained sidewalk.

Whether he returned to the light of the human world, or disappeared forever into the shadows, this had to end.

With a deep breath, Jeremy headed down into the closed-in dimness of the station. The air changed as he descended. The haze of oil and exhaust stayed up on the streets, but a different smell wound up from the platform below—something wild, tinged with the salt of the sea.

He didn't look at the metal rails of the tracks, tried not to think about the darkness they disappeared into.

That morning, he'd woken up knowing what he had to play. The oldest tunes, the eerie modal ones that wept and sang through his cello. The ones that spoke of loss and heartbreak and magics disappearing forever from the world.

He walked past his corner and went right up to the edge of the platform. Quickly, he unfolded his stool, unpacked his cello, and began. An ancient, nameless air to start, the notes vibrating low, soaring up into the high part like a woman weeping. When that tune ended, he moved into a dark, twisty jig called *The Orphan*.

The air in the station stilled. The light shifted, shading to amber. Jeremy looked up at the station sign and his fingers trembled, nearly dropping his bow. Instead of WEST AVENUE the sign now read WIDDERSHINS.

He finished the tune, the last note fading away into a world that was no longer his own.

Gran would tell him to have courage. Jeremy stood, his cello balanced beside him on the slender silver endpin, the embodiment of all his hopes. All his fears. He didn't want to be sitting down when he faced whatever was coming.

A sound issued from the dark tunnel, a high keening that had nothing to do with machinery. Jeremy's pulse throbbed queasily at the back of his throat. Whispering a desperate, useless Hail Mary, he squeezed his eyes closed.

When he opened them again, a train sat at the platform. He hadn't heard it arrive. It resembled the usual A-line cars —white and red, and filled with passengers—but the differences were enough to make his breath tighten in narrowing circles of fear.

He clutched the neck of his cello as if it was the only solid thing in the universe. Oh, he'd set things in motion he had no idea how to end. All he knew was that the fair folk must be faced, or they would drive him to madness.

The train doors silently opened, and the riders stepped out.

Pale maidens with moth-tangled hair, gowned in cobwebs. Twig-jointed creatures with staring eyes. Goblins wearing caps of blood. Sharp-fanged, sinuous hounds. The hollow-eyed banshee. The shambling bog horse.

All the lovely, horrible creatures he had tried not to see his whole life.

And behind them...

Behind them strode a figure clad in midnight. A band of silver encircled his moon-pale hair, and his face was sharp-planed and merciless. Nothing human shone in those starlit eyes.

A shudder crimped Jeremy's spine, and he looked away, wishing he'd brought something—an iron cross, even a handful of salt—to defend himself.

Gran had whispered stories to him once, of the Sidhe lords and ladies gone far to the west, taking their magic with them. The knowledge of what he now faced lodged deep in Jeremy's lungs. He breathed through the stabbing truth of it.

"Jemmy Cahill," the elf-lord said, his voice like frost and famine. "Do you think you can deny us the taste of your music for seven long years without paying a price?"

Swallowing back the sharp tang of fear, Jeremy dug in his pocket and brought out the roll of bills he'd earned busking in the station.

"Here."

The lord laughed, a sound like metal scraping bone. "What use have I for such? You must offer better coin than that."

What else did he have to give? Fingers numb, Jeremy reached beneath his shirt and pulled out Gran's charm. He tugged it from his neck and held it out.

One of the twiggy creatures crept over and snatched it from his hand, and Jeremy flinched back. The watching fair folk laughed, their voices chiming and barking, a cacophony echoed back from the curved ceiling overhead.

The creature delivered the charm to his liege, and the elf-lord held it up, a pathetic scrap of soiled linen and tarnished string.

"A spent ward?" The lord's voice was hollow with fey mirth. "This counts for less than nothing."

He tossed it into the air. A bright flash, the afterimage seared on the inside of Jeremy's eyelids, and Gran's charm was gone.

"Hey! That wasn't fair." Anger made Jeremy straighten, though he couldn't quite look upon the beautiful, terrible face of the elf-lord.

"Do not speak to us of fairness. Is it fair to deny the Sight that runs through your blood? Is it fair to bind your music so tightly it withers to nothing, when we starve to hear it?" At his words, the watching fair folk nodded and murmured. "Your time has run, mortal child. Choose your path."

Jeremy held his cello in front of him like a shield. For a stark moment he considered setting the instrument down and walking away.

Far away, to a place where music didn't matter. Where his soul could shrink and shrivel into normalcy. Where the stuff of nightmares didn't stalk through the shadows of the subway tunnels, or whisper from the corners of alleyways.

The stuff of nightmares.

And dreams. Dark and light entwined, like the night-brilliant lord standing before him, and all his dancing, dreadful court.

Jeremy took a shuddering breath flavored with the scent of the sea. Gran would have wanted him to choose the magic that ran in their shared blood. This was his heritage, his very soul. Clamping his fingers hard around his cello, he met the elf-lord's fathomless gaze.

"I will play for you," Jeremy said. "I will give you my music. Just—don't kill me."

He couldn't simply disappear on his parents. It would break them beyond repair.

Something shivered over the assembled fair folk, trimph and avarice mixed together in the sweet, feral eyes turned upon him.

The lord laughed, his voice resonant with victory. "We have no intentions of ending your mortal life."

Jeremy let out a ragged sigh of relief, but the lord was not finished speaking.

"But when next the moon is full," he said, a fierce light in his eldritch eyes, "you will come join us. Seven years you owe us, mortal, and seven years you shall remain as a bard within our courts. We shall come for you in a fortnight. Be ready."

Seven years? A chill swept over him. Dad could be dead

by then, Mom wasted away by grief. His few friends would forget him, and his career at Juilliard would be completely finished.

Yet the choice had already been made. Gran had always said beware the bargains of the fair folk.

Despite the terror flickering through his veins, something else stirred—a wild and secret joy. He had his music back, and would see magic beyond mortal ken. It was almost worth the price.

The elf-lord turned to leave, and Jeremy lifted his hand.

"Wait!" he cried. "One more thing."

The lord narrowed his bright eyes. "Our business here is done."

"My dad is sick." Jeremy thought furiously. "I'd only play melancholy tunes for you, if I knew he was dying and me not by his side. Can you save him?"

The lord did not reply for a long moment, and Jeremy's heart beat desperately. Please. Please.

"We cannot cure him," the elf-lord said. "But we will ensure he lives until you return to the human world."

It was enough. Jeremy bowed his head.

When he looked up again, the fair folk were gone. Cold air pressed his skin, then heat. Sound returned—the screech of train brakes nearly deafening in the brightly-lit station. He swayed, the taste of starlight and ashes on his tongue.

The crowd, the blessedly human crowd, surged out of the train and headed for the stairs. They brushed past Jeremy, heads bent to screens and phones, heedless.

"You okay, man?" A guy about his age paused and

caught his elbow. "You might want to get your instrument out of the way."

Blinking hard, Jeremy scooted back into the shelter of his corner. He settled on his stool, then toed his upside-down fedora a few inches out. Glancing down at his cello, he caught his breath at the smooth, unmarred surface.

Not everything could be mended by magic, but that wouldn't stop him from trying.

Setting his bow on the strings, he began to play.

GUINEVERE'S GUEST

Originally written for The Uncollected Anthology: Happily
Ever Afters, *this tale is the start of something much bigger. I
haven't had the chance yet to explore the rest of Gwen's story but
it's definitely on my list!*

Halfway through my band's last set, trouble walks
into The Wee Dram Tavern & Eatery. The door opens and
lets in a waft of rain-soaked Portland night—and someone
who's not mortal. I notice right away, even though I'm in
the middle of a song. The feel of a non-human is unmistakable, and my senses are tuned high after playing music
for over two hours.

Nobody else pays him any attention, but then, they
aren't supposed to. That's how Elf glamour works. The guy
isn't wearing leathers or sporting visible scars or animated
tattoos. He's wearing a long dark coat, so he's pretty much

ignored as he gets a pint from the bar and claims a table in the far corner.

I can't get a good look at him—the pub is too dim and the stage lights, pitiful though they are, make it hard to see past the glare focused on the small performing area. The raised dais my band is playing on isn't big enough to merit being called a stage, and the three of us barely fit up here: me in the middle with my Celtic harp, Karen to my right on djmebe, and Danny on the left edge, where his guitar neck won't constantly bang me in the head.

Even though I can't get a clear visual on the guy who just walked in, I can feel him—a metallic prickle along my skin. From what I can sense, he isn't going anywhere. He's watching me. There's a predatory, patient feel to him I don't like. Not that I can do anything about it.

Danny shoots me a look, and we bring the rollicking reel to a close. As the five people actually paying attention clap, he leans over to me.

"You okay, Gwen?" he asks in a low voice.

I nod and pretend to study the set list. Danny knows me a little too well, and I've been careless around him. Not that most humans believe in magic, but musicians tend to be a little more open-minded about weird stuff. I've always made excuses for the things that happen when I use my Bardic power, but Danny isn't buying. At least, not completely.

Earlier that night, in fact, I'd calmed down a couple arguing at the bar. Easy enough when half the songs in our repertoire are love songs. The other half being rowdy drinking songs.

Okay, I lie. Half our songs are covers from the 80s and 90's, which tends to confuse people. They see a Celtic harp, guitar, and African drum and don't expect Madonna and Green Day. It's part of our charm. And part of why we play weekly gigs in dumpy pubs instead of big stages on the festival circuit.

Even if we were wildly commercial, though, I couldn't risk the exposure. A half-trained Bard can't contain the power that playing in front of several thousand people would raise. And if I could control it and *use* it, I'd be in big-ass trouble with the Fey Council. So, either way, I lose.

Thus my somewhat penniless life as a smalltime musician and sometime errand girl for the aforementioned Council. They like to keep tabs on us few humans who possess *real* magic. We're useful for cleaning up small messes, where goblins or other obviously non-human creatures might stand out.

Speaking of standing out, the elf in the corner is doing a good job of passing. He's not even wearing a hooded cloak, Stryder-style.

The band and I play a few more tunes, and I try and block out the elf's presence and just get lost in the music. Finally, we're done for the night.

"Thanks for listening," I say to our small audience. "We're the band Clef. Catch us again next week, and if you enjoyed the music, feel free to leave something in the tip jar."

Usually at this point I send an encouraging nudge toward people's spare change, but with Mister Elf Guy lurking in the back I don't want to risk it. Mortal power is generally disdained as being hardly worth notice by the magical beings in our midst, but you never know what might set one of them off.

Especially the higher-ups, like the Elves and Fae. And the Nightwalkers. Don't ever want to make one of those guys mad, or you'll end up a desiccated corpse at dawn.

The Shifters are a little more chill, but then, many of them were human once, and have some sympathy.

"I can't make it next week," Karen reminds me as she slides her djembe into its case. "The salsa band I play with is doing that out-of-town wedding, and we have to drive on Thursday."

"Right. Have fun—we'll miss you."

Usually I'm the one with the weekend wedding gig. Harps are good for that kind of thing. I finish packing mine away and then tuck the case at the back of the tiny stage. I plan to have a quick chat with the mysterious visitor before grabbing my gear and heading home.

"Hey, Danny." I tap my guitar-player's elbow. "Mind tracking the manager down and getting our pay?"

He glances from me to the figure in the corner.

"Old friend," I lie.

Once the two spotlights are off, I can see the elf in the neon glow of the Guinness sign. His human-seeming face is handsome—elves are vain like that—dark brows slashed over piercing blue eyes, and those killer cheekbones that are every movie cliché. I guess some normal humans *have* seen the fey folk, after all, because those Hollywood depictions get it pretty close.

His pupils are currently round, though, not slitted. His

ears are convincingly rounded, too, from what I can see through his silky blond hair. If I dared to pick up one of those slender, long-fingered hands I bet I'd find the same attention to detail—rounded nails, not the usual claws he can sheathe and unsheathe at will. It's a meticulous disguise, and I wonder why.

As I get close to his table, he nods his head like a lord acknowledging a peasant.

"Guinevere Gaunt, I presume?" he asks.

"Just Gwen." My full name carries way too much history—and power—for me to wear it comfortably. "And you are?"

"Veletherevan T'lorith."

The crazy thing was, that was only part of his name. I could hear all the unsaid syllables behind what he'd given me, trailing like bubbles through the air.

"Um, okay. How about I call you Vel." I almost suggest he pick out a human-sounding name, but decide to save it.

Vel lifts his hand in an elegant gesture. "Please, take a seat."

"You're going to have to work on that," I say, pulling out the second chair and making a show of settling back, booted feet crossed at the ankles. Not as relaxed as I'm pretending to be, of course. I'm already playing close enough to the fire.

"Oh?" He does that super-effective one-eyebrow raise thing.

"The voice. It's too lush. You sound like a Shakesperean actor going overboard."

I see a glint of frost in his blue eyes and he curls his

fingers against the table. Good thing he's pretending to be human, or the wood would sport claw marks.

"I did not come here to bear your insults," he says.

Despite his anger, his voice sounds better. Less like an Elizabethan lord of the deep forest—which is probably the actual truth—and more like a pissed-off human guy.

"Then why are you here?" I ask. "Usually the Council sends a pixie when they want to tell me something."

And boy is that ever a pain. In addition to enduring their hair-pulling and pinching, it's hard to decipher those squeaky little voices. Batting them out of the air and pinning them down doesn't make you any friends among the Greater Fey, though, so I'd learned to tolerate the little pests.

"I am not here on Council business. I am here to retain your services."

I sit up straighter. "What services?"

I mean, it could be anything, and I don't want to give the good-looking elf ideas. Or maybe I do—but that path always ends in tragedy. I know my traditional ballads.

"Are you not Gwen the Harper, available for weddings?" He flicks his fingers and my business card appears between his thumb and index finger, the calligraphed font changing colors in his hand.

"You want to hire me to play a wedding?" I pull my gaze away from the letters flickering purple-red-orange and meet his eyes. My magic tells me he speaks the truth.

He give me a single nod. "My sister's nuptials approach. We are in need of music."

I swallow back sarcasm-laced fear. The short time I'd

spent in the Fae Realm in the past had been enough to convince me I didn't want to hang out there. Or ever visit again. Sure, it was a gorgeous, dreamlike place, but elves were dangerous. Depending on how Dark the particular elves were, hunting mortals for blood sport was considered a fine pastime.

Vel's nostrils flared, like he could smell my surge of adrenaline.

"I need to know more about your House," I say. If he's aligned with the Dark, no way am I setting foot anywhere near that wedding. I probably shouldn't even be considering this. It's best to stay out of Fae business whenever possible.

Of course, I might not have a choice. One doesn't refuse the Fae lightly. I curse my cockiness, sauntering over to his table as if I had nothing to fear.

"House T'lorith follows the path of the Dawn," he says.

I can't help my breath of relief. Dawn is okay. Not as good as Midday, but better than Twilight. And Midnight is flat out. Encounter a Midnight Elf, and you'll be lucky if they finish you off quickly. Being a Dark Fae's plaything is the worst fate I can think of. I'd rather meet a Nightwalker up close.

"But?" I ask. There's something in his voice that puts me on the alert.

Vel's eyes narrow, as if he's pissed I didn't say yes immediately. I look away—I can't help it, the full force of an angry elf's stare is intimidating—then fold my arms and wait.

"There is one thing," he admits. "The House my sister is marrying into is... less aligned with the Light."

Ah, crap. I knew something wasn't right. As if being asked to waltz into the Fae Realm isn't already a perilous thing to do.

"Ever consider calling the wedding off?" I ask.

"It is an alliance our families have been working toward for centuries," he says. "Nothing must mar the ceremony."

"Ah." Understanding prickled up the back of my neck. "Thus the desire for a Bard."

In the ancient days, Bards had the power to soothe enemies and foster an atmosphere of peace. No rulers met without them, no alliances were made, no powerful agreements reached without a Bard present.

If Vel and his family were expecting trouble, I should stay far, far away.

"I'm going to have to decline your offer." I sit up, getting ready to stand and walk away.

The elf waves his index finger, and I'm suddenly glued to the chair.

Ha. Not for long. I hum a little Bob Marley lyric about getting up, and I stand. Vel's eyes widen. Clearly he wasn't expecting a puny little human to break his magic so easily. Of course, if I hadn't just played a full set of music I wouldn't be able to, but he doesn't need to know that.

"Good luck with the wedding," I say.

"Wait." For the first time, his arrogance slips. "Please reconsider. We will triple your usual fee."

I like the hint of vulnerability in his face; it makes him seem more approachable. And frankly, I could use the money. Wedding gigs this time of year tend to dry up, and tip jar earnings are good for ramen and carrots, and not much else.

"I should warn you," I say. "I don't know all the old songs."

Nobody knows all the old Bardic songs of power, not any more. I'd managed to piece some together during my apprenticeship, and my mentors taught me the few ancient chants and tunes they knew, but so much has been lost.

Vel gives me a piercing look. I match his stare.

"As long as you have the talent for peacebringing and soothing," he says, "that will be enough."

"I could do that, yeah. But it might not be pretty."

I *so* should not be agreeing to this. But rent's due next week and, well, hot elf.

And honestly, life as a regular human gets a little boring. It's been a while since the Council sent me on an errand for them, and using my magic to soothe lover's spats and calm irate drunks isn't the most satisfying use of my abilities.

An Elven wedding with a chance for mayhem is a scary prospect, but exhilarating, too. I didn't spend seven years training as a Bard just to spend the rest of my life playing obscure pubs.

"It is a great honor to be asked to attend a Fae wedding," Vel says. His gaze snags mine, holds. "Also, I will personally stand as your protector."

The tone in his voice sends a little thrill through me. I try and ignore it. My own personal Fae warrior...

Let's not go overboard.

It's just a fantasy, anyway. Elf plus human equals tragic ballads, not happy endings.

"I want half the money up front," I say. "Deposited directly into my bank account."

No shenanigans with faerie gold—not that I think Vel would pull something like that. But his leprechaun advisors might, or whatever Lesser Fey his House has handling the mundane details like money.

"Then you accept?" He rises, and I have to tip my chin up to look into his face. Damn, he's tall.

And well-built, with fairly broad shoulders for an Elf. Swordsman maybe, not archer. That's unusual, since metal weapons among the Fae are usually limited to silver daggers and such. Iron, which means steel, is poison to most Fae creatures. Elves included.

The corner of Vel's mouth curls into a nearly invisible smile, as if he's reading my thoughts.

"I have a slight immunity to cold iron," he says. "Thus my role as messenger this evening."

"Right." Totally read my mind—or my face. I need to work on that.

"So." He leans closer, and I smell rain on green leaves and a trace of wood smoke. "We have an agreement?"

Despite my stuttering heart, I give him a cool nod. "We do. I'll play your sister's wedding."

"Good."

He holds out his hand. I stare at it for a second, then realize he wants to shake on the deal. Adopting our strange human customs or something. Bracing myself, I clasp my palm to his.

Something flashes between us at the contact, bright and breathless. I pull my hand away, jerk it away, really, and he does the same. My skin's tingling where it touched his, and I glance at my palm, half expecting to see silvery light shimmering on it. Nothing.

"Well." If an elf can sound shaken, he does. "That was unexpected."

"What *was* that?"

He just stares at me a moment, then shakes his head. "I will come fetch you in time for the wedding."

"Wait." I grab the sleeve of his black trench coat as he turns to leave. "When, exactly, is this event?"

"Tomorrow. I shall arrive at your abode two hours after noon, mortal time. Be ready."

Crap—that gives me like zero preparation time to come up with something to wear, let alone boot up some appropriate lyrics.

"Give a girl some advance notice next time," I say, not bothering to keep the sting from my voice.

"There is never enough time." He gives me an enigmatic smile, then slips out of my grasp like water, strides to the door, and is gone.

"Hey." Danny comes up, cash in his hand. "I finally tracked down the manager and got our pay. Why do they always disappear right at the end of a performance? And speaking of disappearing acts, where'd your visitor go?"

"He had to run." I take my share of the night's profits and fold the bills into my wallet. "You and Karen keep the tips tonight. I got a gig."

"Okay." Danny tilts his head, like he can tell things aren't exactly fine, but he doesn't press.

I appreciate that about him—his ability to accept that sometimes you shouldn't ask questions.

"See you Monday for rehearsal," I say, heading over to pick up my harp.

I hope I'll be around then—and not trapped in the Fae Realm, a casualty of a wedding gone horribly awry.

I WAKE up the next morning in a mild panic. The Fae Realm doesn't care that it's a Friday in the mortal world, just that the moon and stars are aligned—or whatever magical way they decide such things as the proper day to hold a wedding. But that doesn't matter. The real issue is that I have nothing to wear.

Fortunately, it's prom season. I'm at my favorite vintage consignment store the minute they open, coffee in hand from the espresso bar down the corner. The racks are packed with gauzy gowns, and it doesn't take long for me to find a green dress that shows off just the right amount of skin. The skirt is long and flowy, the top a strapless velvet bodice with ribbons in the back. Hopefully it won't be October in the Fae Realm, and I can get by with a wisp of scarf around my shoulders.

Another quick stop at the art supply emporium for flowers and crystals. One hour and a few burned fingers later—hot glue guns suck—I've got something that will work. Yes, the gown looks inelegant and all-too-human, but I can sing a bit of rhyme over it before I head off into fairyland and it will shine with the best of them.

Once my dress is done, I spend the rest of the time before Vel shows up memorizing appropriate songs, and playing tunes to raise my magic.

Here's how it works: I get power from music, and can direct that power by using specific lyrics. Intent matters—I *could* sing gibberish and still cause something to happen—but it's a lot easier when the words are specific.

The catch? I can only use the power of a particular lyric once. Except for the ancient Bardic ballads, which are good for several uses—but those are not to be used lightly. They come with a high cost, too. The one time I sang one, I knocked myself out for three days. Plus there were other complications I really don't want to think about.

Pop songs don't carry that kind of kickback. Older traditional ballads will give me a headache, but they're also more powerful in their execution. Problem is, power in the Fae Realm is like gunpowder. You need to be extra careful, or things will blow up in your face.

Once I have enough Billy Idol and the Cranberries lyrics crammed into my brain, I figure I'm ready. Vel said he'd protect me, right?

Right. Like I trust any Fae to keep me safe.

That's what I have a sharp iron knife for, in case everything goes to hell. I strap on my thigh sheath and slip the blade in, then concentrate on doing my hair. It's currently red—a natural-looking auburn, although I've gone fire-engine in the past. Also blue, purple, and flat black.

When I was born, I was a normal-seeming baby—

except for the silver hair. It took until my sixteenth birthday for the weirdness of my Bardic powers to manifest, but by then I already knew I was *different*. Just how different was brought home when I inadvertently set the high school gym on fire during a choir performance. A week later, I was shipped off to my great aunt in Wales— but that's another story.

At two pm on the dot, Vel knocks on my front door. I let him in, trying not to be overwhelmed by how good he looks. He hasn't bothered with the human disguise this time, and the full force of his Elven appearance is like a punch to the gut.

His face is sharper, his eyes more intense, and a sense of leashed power comes off him in waves. I swallow, glad he's on my side.

He's still wearing the black coat from last night, but underneath I glimpse a velvet doublet embroidered with gold. And, as I suspected, there's a graceful silver sword hung at his side.

"Are you prepared to depart, milady?" he asks, looking me up and down.

My heart thumps loudly under his appraising gaze. I can't tell if he approves of what he sees, and I tell myself I don't care. *Liar.*

"Ready enough," I say, going to grab my harp case.

"One moment." He raises one long finger and dips it into the air, then points at me.

I feel his magic surround me, a breath of rain and smoke. It's a heady sensation, almost like he's caressing me with his hands.

"Hey!" My voice is a little shaky. "No performing enchantments on innocent humans."

That eyebrow goes up. "You are hardly innocent of the ways of the Fae. I am merely assisting with your costume."

I glance down, to see that my dress now glimmers, the fake flowers and cheap crystals transformed to soft blossoms and real gems, with a sprinkling of stardust over the skirt. It's beautiful, and better than what I could have done with my *Roxanne* lyrics.

"I had it handled," I say, still on edge from the touch of his magic. How much does he know about my past, anyway?

"I can remove the effect, if you like." He sounds more amused than offended.

I raise one hand. "It's fine. Leave it." Grudgingly, I add, "You make a good fairy godmother."

His lips twitch up for just a second, and it makes me curious. Who is Veletherevan T'lorith, and why is he comfortable enough with humans that he understands my jokes? Most of the Greater Fae prefer not to sully themselves by spending time in the mortal world. Except those twisted ones who like to torture humans or mess with us in other ways—but I don't feel that kind of darkness inside Vel.

"Okay." I pick up my harp, zipped snugly into its case. "Let's go."

Vel steps over to me and holds out his hand, palm up. "Brace yourself. As soon as we touch, I will transport us."

"Don't you need to make a doorway, or at least go outside or something?" I eye him, and don't take his hand.

I'm not hugely familiar with the ins and out of traveling to the Fae Realm, but it's not as easy as just taking a step through the air and *presto*, arriving in a magical land. The one time I went, it involved an ancient circle of standing stones and quite a bit of preparation.

He gives me a level look. "You are resonant with power, and have trod the path between the worlds before. It is not as complicated as you seem to believe."

"You mean I could accidentally skip over into fairyland, if I'm not careful?" I shiver at the thought.

"No. To cross the boundary takes intent, and the right kind of magic. You will not accidentally stumble into the Realm against your will."

His blue eyes hold understanding, and it confuses me. *Nobody* understands me, and there's no way some high-handed Elf lord should be able to. The more time I spend with Vel the more I like him. And mistrust him.

"All right." I take a deep breath, then reach out and clasp his hand.

Again there's that silvery flash, but it's quickly over-whelmed by a rush of heat as the world tips. I hold tight to my harp and hope I'm not squeezing Vel's hand too hard. I also *really* hope the queasy sensation in my stomach doesn't mean I'm going to be embarrassingly sick once we arrive at our destination

Then the ground under me rights itself. I stumble, and Vel catches me against him, adroitly keeping the harp from banging against his leg. If I were feeling any better, I'd pull away, but it's all I can do to just lean against him and gasp in the herb-scented warmth of the Fae Realm. We're in a glade of silver-barked trees, but I'm too disoriented to take in the details.

"My apologies." His breath tickles my hair. "I expected the crossing to go more smoothly for you. Next time we will be better prepared, and I will not make foolish assumptions."

I blink up at him. Beyond the astonishing fact of an Elf apologizing to a human, there's a genuine look of concern in his eyes.

Oh boy—I should not be falling so fast and so hard. But somehow, with his arms around me and those piercing blue eyes fixed on mine, I can't think.

"What assumptions?" I manage to ask.

Vel's lips twitch downward, as if he's annoyed with himself. "I thought your magic would protect you more fully. You have a rare power, Guinevere. It is easy to forget that you are inexperienced in its use."

His words give me enough small anger that I find the strength to pull away from him. "I've got plenty of experience."

But the reason I'm pissed is that, well, he's speaking the truth. My apprenticeship ended two years ago, and it took me another six months to recover from what happened. Since then, I've been lying low, just popping my head up for the few Fey Council errands, and starting a band.

Part of me knows I've been shying away from the hard truth: I need training and discipline, a way to tame the wild magic inside me before someone decides to use it for themselves. I've already been on that ride, and it wasn't a fun one.

Vel looks like he's about to say something, but a pixie darts up, wings barely visible within its ball of light. It squeaks something high-pitched and Vel nods.

"We must get you settled," he says to me, concern still lingering in his eyes. "The ceremony begins soon."

"Great," I manage. "Lead on."

It's hard not to stare at my surroundings as we walk through the glade. Tall trees with silvery leaves grow evenly spaced apart, and the emerald moss is soft as velvet underfoot. Jewel-bright butterflies flit past, and ahead I glimpse a clearing filled with fey folk.

Elf lords and ladies, beautiful and imperious, make up at least half of the crowd, but the other half is a mix of daydream and nightmare. A faerie maiden with gossamer wings hovers above the ground near a gang of redcap goblins. The smell of flowers and rotting fruit perfumes the air, and the light is strange—a pale radiance that fills the clearing like fog, emanating from everywhere and nowhere. A figure in a dark cloak stands alone, the moss around him dead and brown.

To my relief, I spot one or two humans, though they're probably shifters. The elderly man in long green robes might be a druid, though. Not that I'd rely on any of them for help if I needed it.

Vel tucks my arm through his, guiding me out of the trees and around the edges of the gathering.

A transparent nymph with long fangs turns to stare at me and licks her lips. A hunched troll grumbles to his companion, a creature that looks like a walking shrub. I keep my chin up and try to act confident, as if I stroll through enchanted clearings filled with magical folk every day.

"You are safe here," Vel says softly, as if sensing my thoughts. "Bards are not to be harmed, under any circumstances."

I nod at him, and bite my tongue. Bet I could think of some exceptions.

We halt before an elaborate canopy crafted of vines and flowers. Crystalline lanterns hang from the corners, and the moss beneath is a perfect carpet of emerald green, dotted with starry white blossoms.

"The wedding will take place here," Vel says. "Although —your human word for wedding is a clumsy description at best for this event. It is a binding, a deep, unbreakable alliance."

"That's us humans," I say, not quite keeping the bite out of my voice. "Clumsy at best."

"I did not mean it in such a manner." Vel turns his blue-eyed gaze upon me. "And certainly not in such company as yourself, Guinevere."

"Gwen," I say shortly, disliking the little prickles that go through me when he calls me by my full name.

Already I'm far too attuned to his presence. I don't need the extra help of him calling me by my true and given name. Names have power. I suppose I should be grateful he doesn't know my entire name.

Or maybe he does. The Fey Council has that information.

"You will sit here," he says, indicating a low bench positioned at the side of the wedding canopy.

"Do you want music during the actual ceremony? I don't have much experience with Fae weddings. Bindings. Whatever."

"No—we have our own traditions. Your job is to keep the gathering in a soothed and peaceable mood."

I glance over at a group of elves dressed in garments black as night. When they move, their clothing sparkles as though stitched with stars. Their hair is black—onyx sheened with indigo—and their features are even more severe and brutally gorgeous than Vel's. The place they stand seems shadowed, dimmer than the surrounding air. *Dammit.* Midnight Elves.

I send up a prayer to any power that might be listening that *he* won't be here.

One of them looks over, as if sensing my gaze. His silver eyes meet mine and a wave of dizziness hits me. I hear chimes, and ice crawls up my spine.

"Gwen." Vel takes my arm and turns me to face him. "Do not stare at those that walk in midnight."

"I know." I shiver. "Really, I do know that."

Brows drawn together, he shifts his grasp and takes my hand. Before I even know what he's doing, he brings the back of my hand up and presses a kiss on it.

Heat and warmth flare from the contact, and I'm dizzy again, but in a far different way. I can feel the blood surging through me, a blush lighting my cheeks. He holds my hand for two heartbeats, three, then releases me.

It's all I can do not to stumble back. The effect of the Midnight Elves is gone—banished by Vel's touch and whatever magic is in his kiss.

"How long will this ceremony take?" I ask, trying to keep my voice casual, like handsome elf warriors kissed my hand every day. No biggie.

"Long enough." Vel lifts one shoulder in a shrug. "Time is fluid in the Realm, as I think you know."

I do know—not only from personal experience, but all the ballads and tales. Rip Van Winkle spending a night with the fairies and coming back one hundred years later is only one example of many.

Though in my experience, the reverse was true: a month in the Fae Realm only took the length of an afternoon in the human world. Too bad my mentors hadn't realized I'd been gone so long, until almost too late...

I slam a mental door on my memories, and concentrate on unpacking my harp.

"I'll start playing now, then," I tell Vel. "If that's okay."

Might as well begin sooner rather than later. That way I'll have a bit of power raised, just in case. I don't let myself consider what that case might be.

"Yes," he says. "I will remain nearby."

I'm glad to hear it. Settling on the bench, I resolutely keep my gaze away from the dark-clad elves. *They can't hurt me.* I hope.

Best to start with something older, steeped in tradition. In homage to the situation, I play some Turlough O'Carolan tunes—the last great Irish Bard, who was said to have been gifted with music by the faeries. The sweet notes waft over the clearing, and the subtle tension humming through the gathering notches down.

Partway through my third piece, a whisper flutters

through the nearby forest. The leaves shimmer, silver, green, silver, and I know without being told that the ceremony is about to begin. When the tune comes full circle, I pluck a final chord and let the notes fade away like ripples in a pond.

To my right, the grove of trees is filled with the brightness of Dawn, while to my left a shadow clings, dark stars shining beneath. I rest my hands on the wood of my harp, finished for the moment, but ready to play again at a moment's notice. The magic I've raised vibrates inside my chest, waiting.

A creature appears beneath the canopy of vines and flowers—a pure white stag with antlers of ivory. Beside him a figure in a hooded black cloak materializes. I can't quite see its face, and I'm not sure I want to. Power radiates from it—starlight and roses and a hint of decay.

The brightness and darkness move toward the clearing, until there's a clear line in the middle of the forest where Midnight meets Dawn. Then an elf maiden steps from beneath the shelter of the trees, and I catch my breath.

Her golden hair falls unbound to her knees, and she's wearing a dress made of rose-gold light. There's no other way to describe it—it's like she pulled down some of the aurora and wrapped it about herself just at sunrise.

She's the kind of perfectly gorgeous that makes me want to weep with joy and despair. I feel coarse and ungainly, my fingers too thick, my features too ugly and human. The only thing I have that can compare is my hair, and it's hidden behind a layer of dye and hacked off to a practical length.

On the spot, I decide to let it grow out and return to its natural moonsilver color.

Behind the bride come a dozen fey handmaidens, mostly elves, though one or two sport gossamer wings, and I think there's a nixie in the way back.

Then the groom enters the glade, and the light fades.

His black hair pulls the light, and his eyes are midnight holes, sucking everything in. He's wearing dark velvet stitched with silver embroidery and amethysts. Behind him pace a dozen male fae, including a Nightwalker. There's no mistaking the deathly pallor of the creature.

Despite myself, I shiver—and Vel's hand comes to rest on my shoulder, warm and comforting.

Never thought I'd be grateful for an elf's touch, but that's the second time today. I hate to think there might be a third, but these kinds of things come in threes.

The couple walk forward until they are face to face. Slowly, she raises her right hand. In a mirror gesture, he raises his left. The light flickers wildly. When their palms touch, there's a deep ringing sound, as though an enormous bell has just been struck.

"Come," the cloaked figure beside the stag says. "Say the words of the binding, with myself and the White Hart as witness, and this long-awaited union shall be complete."

Hands clasped, the couple walks forward until they stand beneath the canopy. I keep my head bowed, only watching with my peripheral vision. Between the bride's heartrending beauty and the groom's terrifying features, they're too dangerous to look at.

Light and shadow course over the gathered crowd,

warm, then cold. I feel dizzy. Only Vel's touch on my shoulder keeps me from swaying.

That, and the solid wood of my harp against my collar-bone, the comforting small buzz of magic in my belly.

"Twined together, dark and light, from the morning to the night," the bride and groom say in unison. Their voices pulse and echo through the clearing. "From this binding there shall be two houses bound in fealty."

"Drink." The cloaked figure holds out an ornate silver goblet studded with moonstones.

The bride takes it and lifts it to her lips.

The white stag flares its nostrils, and a waft of something sickly-sweet reaches my nose.

Before I can call out a warning, the elf maiden sips, then crumples to the ground, her gown a pool of light around her. The goblet tumbles down, dark liquid spreading over the moss like a stain.

"Traitor!" Vel cries.

Unsheathing his sword, he leaps toward the bride-groom. The dark elf twists, a blade of shadow appearing in his hand. The clang of their swords meeting shakes the silver leafed-trees. Blossoms rain down from the wedding canopy, falling over the handmaidens and other folk surrounding the fallen bride.

Panic rises in my chest. My magic's not strong enough to counter this kind of killing violence. Even if I could make my trembling hands play a note, I know nobody would hear me through the cries of panic, the harsh wind shaking the trees.

I have to get out of here. I'm a mere mortal, surrounded

by fae folk who could strike me down with a breath, and my protector is currently engaged in what looks to be a battle to the death.

But I don't know how to get back to the mortal world by myself. *Dammit.*

One of the Midnight Elves attending the ceremony turns to look at me, and my heart clenches. *No. Oh no.*

I recognize those eyes—cold sapphires I once drowned in. As I watch, he drops the glamour concealing his true face, and I shiver. Lurching up, I grab my harp and desperately glance around for a safe place to hide.

There is no safe place. There is no escape from *him.* Before I can blink, he's standing before me, lips curved in a deadly smile.

"Guinevere," he says, his voice claiming my name. "I always knew you would return to me."

The worst thing is that part of me yearns for him, like an addict craving her drug. My stomach knots as I struggle against that darkness inside me. I defeated it once, I can do it again.

"I'm not yours," I say. My voice comes out shaky. I'm prey, and he's the hunter.

"Of course you are." He reaches out and lightly runs his sharp-nailed fingers down my cheek. At the last second, he presses in.

I wince at the sharp sting as he draws blood, then almost retch when he brings his fingers to his mouth.

"Delicious," he murmurs, licking the trace of my blood off his nails. "I can hardly wait to savor the sweetness of your death. The delay will make it all the more satisfying."

I force myself not to sway toward him. Yes, he'll kill me, but first he'll toy and torture, bespelling me so that I find each cut exquisite, each pain sweeter than the last.

"Gwen!" Vel calls out. "Run, seek my family!"

I glance over, to see him staring at me. It's a fatal inattention. Horrified, I watch as the bridegroom sweeps his blade toward Vel's neck.

NO.

It won't end like this. I won't let it.

Wrenching my attention to my harp, I drop to my knees on the soft ground and strike a chord. All my fear, all my anger, pours into the music. I open myself to the magic in my blood, and somehow sense the power of the Fae Realm pouring into me, too.

Hammering my fingers on the notes, I start playing the only song I can think of that will save us. Billy Idol's White Wedding.

My voice is harsh as I scream out the words of the chorus, each one gathering in strength, until I reach the important phrase, "… to start again!"

I wail the last word like a banshee, drawing the vowels out, forcing them over the clearing, over the gathered fae, over the white stag and the hooded figure. Somehow, I can taste my own blood in my mouth. I feel the connection between myself and my midnight enemy. Wrapping the force of my will around that thread, I pull, hard.

Dark power courses through me. I see his eyes widen. I see the white hart leap into the air, flying. I see the indigo-cloaked figure standing beneath the canopy begin to pull back her hood with pale, long-fingered hands.

"Take me home," I sing, still channeling the raw power of Billy Idol. The words sear my throat.

The world tips. I smell roses and frost. Wrapping my arms around my harp, I hold on tight as everything dissolves around me.

Cold slices into me. I can't breathe, can't think. *Home*, I think desperately. *Take me home.*

Then I crash land into the middle of my living room floor. Twisting, I curl over to protect my harp, landing so hard on my back that I nearly black out. I'm freezing. My dress and hair are covered with frost that immediately begins to melt.

I lie there gasping, trying to clear the bright spots from my vision. The wood of my harp digs into my abdomen, and pretty soon I'm lying in a small puddle of chilly water.

"Get up," I say to myself. The words scrape out hoarsely, and feel like I'm regurgitating sandpaper. Right. Don't talk.

Slowly, I move my harp off me and manage to sit up, suppressing a groan. I feel like I've been run over by a post-apocalyptic tank with spiked tires. The room spins crazily, and the puddle of water on the floor seems like an appealing bed. I don't know how I'm going to make it to my feet without keeling right over again.

A rush of light and chiming bells, and Vel is suddenly kneeling beside me, one strong arm around my shoulders.

"Gwen." He says my name like it's important to him. "Are you well?"

"Not really." I lean against him, grateful for the support. "Are you?"

At least his head is still attached, and there doesn't seem to be a gaping wound anywhere on his body.

"I am physically uninjured," he says, literal as ever. "But my magic has been temporarily leeched."

"How?" I didn't even know that was a thing.

He just stares at me, his blue eyes intense, as if I had something to do with that.

"No. Oh no." I remember pulling power to me. Dark power, and bright. I scoot back a little, then moan as the movement sets off a chain reaction of hurt.

"You need to be resting." Mouth set, he scoops me up in his arms like I weigh nothing more than a blanket.

"You're getting wet," I protest, but my heart's not in it. Bed sounds like a good idea.

"That is easily dealt with."

He flicks his fingers, and moisture wicks out of my dress and hair instantly, which helps.

"You should patent that," I say drowsily. "Make a fortune."

"Shh."

He strides over to my bed, and I'm too tired to be embarrassed that it's barely made—the down comforter pulled up in a half-assed fashion, the pillow sideways. When he sets me down I sigh, then begin to shiver.

Muttering curses that must be in Elvish, they sound so beautiful, he tugs the comforter up around me. A moment later the bed dips a little with his weight. I don't know how to react to that—my thoughts have turned sludgy and slow. The last thing I notice before I crash into sleep is the feel of his arm around my waist, pulling me close against the warmth of his body...

THAT MUST HAVE BEEN a hell of a party, I think, prying open my sleep-glued eyelids. I feel like roadkill left out in the late November rain.

Then memory returns like an electric shock, zapping me fully awake.

The wedding. The attack. Vel.

Slowly, I turn my head. He's still there, gorgeous eyes closed, chest rising and falling slowly as he sleeps.

Damn. I've got an elf in my bed. Every girl's dream.

Despite his assurances that he was unharmed, I study him closely. He's still wearing his wedding finery, and I don't see any rips or bloodstains. Best of all, his strong throat is unmarked. That blade poised to kill him didn't land, and once again I wonder what happened.

Of course he opens his eyes as I'm leaning over, staring at him.

"Um, hi," I say as heat flushes into my cheeks. "Just checking."

One dark eyebrow goes up, but he doesn't leap out of bed. "And?"

"You seem okay." I flop back down onto my pillow, then regret it as my head starts to pound.

"I told you, I was not hurt in the fight. What did you do, Guinevere Gaunt, to change the course of fate so drastically?"

"I changed fate?" Whoo boy. Goosebumps run up my arms at the thought. "I don't think I can do that, actually. I'm just—"

"There is more to you than anyone suspected." Now it's his turn to go up on one elbow and regard me. His stare is piercing, as though he wants to drill down and discover all the secrets in my soul.

Clearly there are a few more secrets there than even *I* know about, if what he says is true. I changed fate? It's a horrifying, exhilarating thought.

"Are you sure it was me? I mean, there were a lot of magical beings in that clearing. I don't think I'm strong enough to budge sunlight, let alone turn fate."

"You alone do not have the power. But somehow you were able to tap into other sources."

"You?" I whisper, recalling what he said about having his magic drained.

I remember latching onto *him*, too, my midnight shadow. And did I really tap into the magic of the Fae Realm somehow? No wonder I feel like crap.

"Among others. You can be sure that the Fey Council is now *extremely* interested in you and your powers."

Closing my eyes, I groan. What am I, some sort of magic-sucking vampire?

A feather-light touch on my cheek makes me open my eyes. He's patted his hand against my face, in comfort and sympathy.

"You act pretty human, for an elf," I say.

The skin around his eyes tightens for a moment, and I sense some old, deep pain there.

"Anyway," I change the subject, "I have no idea how or what I did at the wedding"—except channel some Billy Idol—"so I have no way to repeat it. Everyone can stop worrying about me."

Right. Like that was going to happen. Even an ignorant human like me knew that this was some big-ass magic. Changing fate, even a little. Damn.

As if reading my thoughts, he gives me a rueful half smile. "Gwen, leaving you to go your own way is not possible. The Fey Council is sending you a guardian while you regain your strength, and to accompany you during your training sessions in the Fae Realm."

"I'm not going back there!" I sit up and grab my pillow, hugging it to my chest. A pit opens in my stomach, and I swallow back nausea at the thought.

"You must." His voice is gentle. "Power like yours cannot go untrained, unexplored. Now that it is fully awoken, it will burn you up from the inside."

"I don't want it. I never wanted this." Why can't I just be a normal girl, with a steady boyfriend and a quirky job?

I don't realize a tear has slipped down my face until he lays a finger against my cheek and catches it. It glistens there, a tiny, perfect sphere of grief.

"May I sip your sorrow?" he asks. "It will help restore me."

Wordlessly, I nod. If my tears will help give back the power I stripped from him, I'm glad to offer them.

He raises his finger to his lips and tastes the droplet. Instantly, a touch more color returns to his eyes. Wrapped in my own misery, I hadn't realized how washed-out he'd looked until that moment.

"What else can I do?" I ask.

He shakes his head. "I will regain my magic well enough over the next few days."

"This is crazy. I mean, you practically died, and I did who-knows-what with my powers. I don't even know who I am anymore, and the Fey Council is going to send somebody, probably any second—"

"Shh." He brings one hand up and cups my cheek. "I do not understand it either, but there is one thing I am sure of. Fate has twined us together, Guinevere Gaunt. As for the guardian the Council is sending, he is already here."

It takes me a second, and then I blink at him. "Wait. You're my guardian?"

"Yes." His expression is somber. "I hope this is not troubling to you."

Oh, it's troubling all right—but mostly in a good way. I mean, if I have to wrestle with newly unlocked powers and have somebody watching over me night and day, I'd far prefer a nice-guy elf to one of the other fae creatures.

Particularly *this* elf.

What Vel said is true; there's a connection between us. Even before I stole his magic, I think we both felt it.

"Okay." I give him a weary grin. "You can stay."

I don't really have a choice. I mean, the Fey Council already made their decision and I don't have the ability to overturn it, even if I wanted to. A girl had to have some pride though, you know?

"I will do my best to keep from interfering in your daily life," he says.

"Interfere all you want."

I can admit, if only to myself, that I was getting a little bored and lonely, with the one bright spot in my week being the Thursday gig at The Wee Dram. Having Vel around will certainly make things more interesting. In all kinds of ways.

My mind skitters away from the "going back to the Fae Realm for more training" part. I'm not ready—the idea of it makes me feel sick.

As if sensing my thoughts, Vel pulls me close against him. I can hear his heartbeat next to my ear.

"We both need to regain our strength," he says. "I will prepare a sleeping pallet in the other room."

I hold on to him tight, not quite ready for him to share my bed, but not ready to let go.

"Just stay with me for a bit," I say as a wave of tiredness crashes over me.

"Whatever you ask." His breath stirs my hair. "Lie down, and I will hold you until you sleep."

It's the best offer I've gotten in a long time. Mutely, I nod and settle back down, my head on the pillow. He gathers me close his touch tender and strong at the same time.

I fall asleep in his arms, feeling safer than I have in years.

∾

THE SCENTS of bacon and coffee tickle my nose, and I wake up. Vel's not in the bed any more, but the noises coming from the kitchen reassure me that he's still around. Plus the delicious smell. I lie there a minute, assessing. My head doesn't hurt, and I'm not slamming up against the edge of exhaustion any more, though I'm still tired. Gingerly, I reach inside, into that place the bardic magic gathers.

It's empty, of course. Even if I'd gone to bed with a reservoir of power, it would have seeped away as I slept.

I'm afraid of trying to summon more. Later. After breakfast and Vel and I figure out the whole roommate thing.

I never thought I'd be sharing space with one of the fae, let alone an elf lord. How is this even going to work?

Vel peeks into the bedroom, his eyes smiling when he sees I'm awake.

"Stay there," he says.

"Okay." I push some pillows behind my back and sit up, noticing that my ruined gown has become a cotton nightgown.

I blush a little at the thought of Vel using his magic to give me something to sleep in. He returns, carrying a tray with a plate of bacon and eggs, toast, a sliced orange, and coffee.

Wow. I could get used to this.

"That looks delicious," I say as he sets the tray down on the bedside table. "Join me?"

"I do not need mortal food," he says, though he comes to sit next to me on the bed.

"What, you live on flower nectar?" I wave a piece of bacon under his nose. "How can you resist this?

He leans forward and takes a bite of the bacon. His teeth are a little too sharp for a mortal, but they don't bother me. None of him bothers me—at least not in a scary way.

I take a long drink of coffee, glad to find that Vel clearly knows his way around a coffee maker as well as a frying pan. Plus he put exactly the right amount of cream in.

Suddenly ravenous, I demolish my breakfast in about two minutes flat. Or maybe I'm just trying to put off the discussion that Vel and I need to have.

I set the empty plate back on the tray and sit up a little further in bed. Funny, I'm not as embarrassed about having this conversation wearing a nightgown as I probably should be. Despite Vel's leashed, predatory power, I feel less threatened by him now. Maybe the fact that I was able to tap into and drain that power makes the difference. I'm not just a defenseless human any more, even though I have no idea how I did what I did.

Also, I trust him. Maybe more than I should.

"So," I say. "We need to talk about the fact that you're now my long-term guest."

"Is this acceptable to you?" His blue eyes gaze into mine.

I try and ignore the little shiver that goes through me as I meet his eyes. "It's not like I have a choice. And frankly, I'd way rather have you as my guardian than some nasty goblin."

"I don't know how long this arrangement will be necessary." There's a hint of apology in his eyes. "It might be for a rather extended time."

We can make this work. Somehow.

"If you get on my nerves too much, I'm banishing you to the shed," I say.

One eyebrow goes up. "You have a shed?"

"Not yet—but something can be arranged." I'm pretty sure it won't come to that. "I hope you have some kind of magical closet. You've probably noticed my place is pretty small."

I was lucky to find this tiny one-bedroom cottage for rent, tucked behind the main house in a decent residential neighborhood. My landladies are two nice older women who've clearly been together for a long time. They do me the favor of not asking too many questions, and I pay my rent on time and keep the place relatively tidy.

I hoped they won't mind my new "friend" taking up residence.

"I do not need much space," Vel said. "A place for my weapons chest. A sleeping pallet."

"I could get a bigger couch. Maybe a pullout. And you should be prepared to pay a little extra for rent." No guarantee my landladies wouldn't raise it a little. I would, in their place.

He nodded. "I am prepared to do whatever is necessary to not impinge upon your life, Gwen."

"Yeah, it's a little late for that." I smile at him, to take some of the sting out of the words.

May your life be interesting is supposed to be a mild curse, but I don't think a boring existence is anything to celebrate either. For the first time in two years, I feel like the fog has lifted. There's a lightness inside my chest that makes it a little easier to breathe, and after a minute I finally can put a name to the sensation.

Hope. And the knowledge that maybe my power can be used for good, after all.

Even though I didn't save Vel's sister, I managed to save him. I changed fate. That's worth something.

He leans forward, a serious look on his handsome face. "I regret bringing this upheaval into your life."

"I don't."

To my surprise, it's true.

∼

ICE IN D MINOR

First appearing in Timberland Writes Together, *this story takes a look at one of the biggest issues facing our modern world, and imagines one possible solution...*

RINNA SEN PACED BACKSTAGE, TUCKING HER MITTENED hands deep into the pockets of her parka. The sound of instruments squawking to life cut through the curtains screening the front of the theater: the sharp cry of a piccolo, the heavy thump of tympani, the whisper and saw of forty violins warming up. *Good luck with that.* Despite the huge heaters trained on the open-air proscenium, the North Pole in February was *cold.*

And about to get colder, provided she did her job.

The stage vibrated slightly, balanced in the center of a parabolic dish pointed straight up to the distant specks of stars in the frigid black sky. The stars floated impossibly far away—but they weren't the goal. No, her music just had to reach the thermo-acoustic engine hovering ten miles above the earth, centered over the pole.

Rinna breathed in, shards of cold stabbing her lungs. Her blood longed for summer in Mumbai; the spice-scented air that pressed heat into skin, into bone, so deeply a body wanted to collapse under the impossible weight and lie there, baking, under the blue sky.

That had been in her childhood. Now, nobody lived in the searing swath in the center of the globe. The heat between the tropics had become death to the human organism.

Not to mention that her home city was now under twenty feet of water. There was no going back, ever.

"Ms. Sen?" Her assistant, Dominic Larouse, hurried up, his nose constantly dripping from the chill. "There's a problem with the tubas."

Rinna sighed—a puff of breath, visible even in the dim air. "What, their lips are frozen to the mouthpieces? I told them to bring plastic ones."

"Valve issues, apparently."

Dominic dabbed his nose with his ever-present hand-kerchief. He'd been with her for two years, and she still couldn't break through his stiff formality. But little things, like insisting on being called by her first name, weren't worth the aggravation. Not here, not now.

"Get more heaters on them," she said, "and tell those damn violins we start in five minutes, whether they're warmed up or not."

"Five minutes. Yes ma'am."

Her job included being a hardass, but she knew how difficult it was to keep the instruments on pitch. The longer they waited, the worse it would get.

Goddess knew, they'd tried this the easy way by feeding remote concerts into the climate engine. Ever since the thing was built, the scientists had been trying to find the right frequencies to cool the atmosphere. They'd had the best luck with minor keys—something about the energy transfer—and at first had tried running synthesized pitches through. Then entire performances. Mozart's Requiem had come close, but not close enough.

It had to be a live performance; the immediate, present sounds of old wood, horsehair, brass and felt, the cascade of subtle human imperfection, blown and pulled and pounded from the organic bodies of the instruments.

There was no substitute for the interactions of sound waves, the immeasurable atomic collisions of an on-site concert fed directly into the engine. Once the thing got started, the techs had promised they could loop the sound. Which was good, because no way was Rinna giving up the rest of her life to stand at the North Pole, conducting a half-frozen orchestra. Not even to save the planet.

She'd spent years working on her composition, assembled the best symphony in the world, rehearsed them hard, then brought them here, to the Arctic. Acoustic instruments and sub-zero temperatures didn't get along, but damn it, she'd make this happen.

What if the composition is a failure? The voice of all her doubts ghosted through her thoughts, sounding suspiciously like her long-dead father.

She pinned it down and piled her answers on top, trying to smother it into silence.

The simulations had proven that certain frequencies played through the engine could super-cool the air over the pole. Then, with luck, a trickle-down effect would begin and slowly blanket the world. The scientists had run the models over and over, with a thousand different types of sound. But it wasn't until the suits had hired Rinna—one of the best composers in the world (not that the world cared much about symphonies)—that the project had really started to gel.

"Ms. Sen." Dominic hurried up again, holding out the slim screen of her tablet. "Vid call for you."

"I told you, I don't want any interruptions."

"It's the President."

"Oh, very well." Fingers clumsy through her mittens, Rinna took the call.

President Nishimoto, Leader of the Ten Nations of the World, smiled at her through the clear, bright screen. Behind him, the desert that used to be Moscow was visible through the window of his office.

"Ms. Sen," he said. "The entire world wishes you the very best of luck in your performance."

He didn't need to say how much was at stake. They all knew.

"Thank you." She bowed, then handed the screen back to Dominic.

It was almost too late. Last winter, the pole ice had thinned so much it couldn't support the necessary installation. Doom criers had mourned the end, but a freak cold-snap in January had given them one final chance.

Now here they were—the orchestra, the techs, Rinna. And five thousand brave, stupid souls, camping on the precarious ice. Come to see the beginning of the world, or the end of it.

Out front, the oboe let out an undignified honk, then found the A. Rinna closed her eyes as the clear pitch rang out, quieting the rest of the musicians. The violins took it up, bows pulling, tweaking, until there was only one perfect, single note. It deepened as the lower strings joined in, cellos and basses rounding the A into a solid arc of octaves.

She could feel the dish magnifying the vibration, up through her feet. Sound was powerful. Music could change the world. She had to believe that.

As the strings quieted, Rinna stripped off her mittens, then lifted her conductor's baton from its velvet-lined case. The polished mahogany grip was comfortable in her hand, despite the chill. The stick itself was carved of mammoth ivory, dug out of the ground centuries ago.

She ran her fingers up and down the smooth white length. It was fitting, using a relic of an extinct animal in this attempt to keep humans from going out the same way.

She stepped onstage, squinting in the stage lights, as the wind instruments began to tune. First the high silver notes of the flutes, then the deep, mournful call of the French horns and low brass. Sounded like the tubas had gotten themselves sorted out.

From up here, the ice spread around stage—not pale

and shimmering under the distant stars, but dark and clotted with onlookers. Originally, she'd imagined performing to the quiet, blank landscape—but that was before some brilliantly wacko entrepreneur had started selling tickets and chartering boats into the bitter reaches of the North.

The concert of a lifetime, plus the novelty of cold, drew spectators from all over the planet. No doubt the thrill of the chill had worn off, but the performance, the grand experiment, was still to come.

And truthfully, Rinna was glad for the crowd. Thermo-acoustics aside, she knew from long experience that the energy of playing in front of responsive listeners was *different*. Call it physics, call it woo-woo, but the audience was an integral part of the performance.

The project director had been reluctant at first, constructing only a small shelter and selling tickets at prices she didn't even want to contemplate. The enclosed seating held roughly forty people: heads of state, classical music aficionados, those with enough money and sense to try and stay warm. But when the boats started arriving, the tents going up, what could he do?

The spectators all wanted to be here, with the possible exception of Dominic hovering beside the podium.

The crowd caught sight of her striding across the stage, and applause rushed like a wind over the flat, frigid plain. She lifted her hand in acknowledgement. Over-head, the edge of the aurora flickered, a pale fringe of light.

Rinna stepped onto the podium and looked over her

orchestra, illuminated by white spotlights and the ruddy glow of the heaters.

She'd bribed and bullied and called in every favor owed her, and this was the result. The best symphony orchestra the entire world could offer. Rehearsals had been the Tower of Babel: Hindi, Chinese, English, French—over a dozen nationalities stirred together in a cacophonous soup. But the moment they started playing, they had one perfect language in common.

Music.

The orchestra quieted. One hundred and five pairs of eyes fixed on her, and Rinna swallowed back the quick burst of nausea that always accompanied her onto the podium. The instant she lifted her baton and scribed the downbeat, it would dissipate. Until then, she'd fake feeling perfectly fine.

"Dominic?" she called, "are the techs ready?"

"Yes," he said.

"Blow your nose." No point in marring the opening with the sound of his sniffles.

Pasting a smile on her face, Rinna turned and bowed to the listeners spread out below the curve of the stage. They applauded, sparks of excitement igniting like distant fire-crackers.

She pulled in a deep breath, winced as the air stabbed her lungs, and faced the orchestra—all her brave, dedicated musicians poised on the cusp of the most important performance of their lives.

The world premiere of *Ice*.

The air quieted. Above the orchestra a huge amplifier

waited, a tympanic membrane ready to take the sound and feed it into the engine, transmute it to frigidity.

Rinna raised her arms, and the musicians lifted their instruments, their attention focused on her like iron on a magnet. She was their true north. The baton lay smoothly in her right hand—her talisman, her magic wand. If there ever was wizardry in the world, let it come to her now.

Heart beating fast, she let her blood set the tempo and flicked her stick upward. Then down, irrevocably down, into the first beat of *Ice*.

A millisecond of silence, and then the violins slid up into a melodic line colored with aching, while the horns laid down a base solid enough to carry the weight of the stars. The violas took the melody, letting the violins soar into descant. The hair on the back of her neck lifted at the eerie balance. Yes. Perfect. Now the cellos—too loud. She pushed the sound down slightly with her left hand, and the section followed, blending into the waves of music that washed up and up.

Rinna beckoned to the harp, and a glissando swirled out, a shimmering net cast across dark waters. Was it working? She didn't dare glance up.

High overhead, the thermo-acoustic engine waited, the enormous tubes and filters ready to take her music and make it corporeal—a thrumming machine built to restore the balance of the world.

It was crazy. It was their best chance.

Ice was not a long piece. It consisted of only one movement, designed along specific, overlapping frequencies. Despite its brevity, it had taken her three years to compose, working with the weather simulations and the best scientific minds in the world. Then testing on small engines, larger ones, until she stood here.

Now Rinna gestured and pulled, molded and begged, and the orchestra gave. Tears glazed her vision, froze on her lashes, but it didn't matter. She wasn't working from a score; the music lived in her body, more intimately known to her than her own child.

The clarinets sobbed the melody, grieving for what was already lost. The polar bears. The elephants. The drowned cities. The silenced birds.

Now the kettle-drums, a gradual thunder—raising the old magic, working up to the climax. The air throbbed and keened as Rinna rose onto her toes and lifted her hands higher. Higher. A divine plea.

Save us.

Arms raised high, Rinna held the symphony in her grasp, squeezed its heart for one more drop of musical blood. The musicians gave, faces taut with effort, shiny with sweat even in the chill. Bows flew, a faint sparkle of rosin dust flavoring the air. The trumpets blared, not missing the triad the way they had in rehearsal.

The last note. Hold. Hold. Hold.

She slashed her hand through the air and the sound stopped. *Ice* ended, yearning and dissonant, the final echo ringing into the frigid sky.

Above, nothing but silence.

Rinna lowered her arms and rocked back on her heels. From the corner of her eye, she saw the techs gesturing frantically, heads shaking, expressions grim.

The bitter taste of failure crept into her mouth, even as the crowd erupted into shouts and applause, a swell of sound washing up and over the open stage. She turned and gave them an empty bow, then gestured to the symphony— the musicians who had given and given. For nothing.

They stood, and one over-exuberant bassoonist let out a cheer and fist-pump. It sent the rest of the orchestra into relieved shouts, and she didn't have the heart to quiet them. They began stamping their feet, the stage vibrating, humming, low and resonant.

Rinna caught her breath, wild possibility flickering through her.

She gestured urgently to the basses. Three of them began to play, finding the note, expanding it. The rest of the section followed, quickly joined by the tubas—bless the tubas. Rinna opened her arms wide, and the string players hastily sat and took up their instruments again.

"D minor!" she cried. "Build it."

The violins nodded, shaping harmonies onto the note. The harpist pulled a trembling arpeggio from her strings, the wind instruments doubled, tripled the sound into an enormous chord buoyed up by breath and bone, tree and ingot, hope and desperation.

The stage pulsing beneath her, she turned to the crowd and waved her arms in wide arcs.

"Sing!" she yelled, though she knew they couldn't hear her.

The word hung in a plume before her. She could just make out the upturned faces below, pale circles in the endless Arctic night.

Slowly, the audience caught on. Sound spread like ripples from the stage, a vast buzzing that resolved into pitch. Rinna raised her arms, and the volume grew, rising up out of five thousand throats, a beautiful, ragged chorus winging into the air.

Beneath their feet, the last of the world's ice began to hum.

The techs looked up from their control room, eyes wide, as high overhead the huge engine spun and creaked.

Rinna tilted her face up, skin stiff as porcelain from the cold, and closed her eyes. She felt it, deep in her bones, a melody singing over and over into the sky. The thrum of sound transformed to super-cooled air, the long hard pull back from the precipice.

Something touched her face, light as feathers, insubstantial as dreams.

Quietly, perfectly, it began to snow.

ACKNOWLEDGMENTS

Thank you for reading my collection of tales! I hope you enjoyed the magical, musical journeys contained therein.

I'd like to thank Kris Rusch and Dean Wesley Smith for helping put my feet firmly on the path of short story writing. Without them and their workshops, many of these tales would never have been written, and I would not have had nearly as much fun playing in the world of short fiction.

Thanks, too, to all my indie author pals who keep me sane and productive, especially the WoUF gals.

And special thanks to my cover designer, Ravven, for yet another lushly gorgeous cover. You're fabulous!

If you'd like to keep up with me, please join my mailing list. I send out monthly newsletters announcing new releases, sales, and reader goodies. Sign up at antheasharp.com

COMETS & CORSETS

THE DARKWOOD CHRONICLES

Deep in the Darkwood, a magical doorway leads to the enchanted and dangerous land of the Dark Elves~

ELFHAME

HAWTHORNE

RAINE

SHORT STORY COLLECTIONS

TALES OF FEYLAND & FAERIE

TALES OF MUSIC & MAGIC

THE FAERIE GIRL & OTHER TALES

THE PERFECT PERFUME & OTHER TALES

COFFEE & CHANGE

MERMAID SONG

Growing up, Anthea Sharp spent most of her summers raiding the library shelves and reading, especially fantasy. She now makes her home in the sunny Southern California, where she writes, plays the fiddle, and writes up a storm. Visit her website at antheasharp.com, friend her on Facebook, and be the first to know about new releases and reader perks by subscribing to her new release newsletter.